Kids Love Hannah Smart: Operation Josh Taylor!

"… I would really like to read this book again, and again, and again." — Leilia

"I absolutely loved the funny parts in the book and I would love for the second book to have humorous parts too … you are an awesome writer." — Charlotte

"I recommend that you make a second book … your book was so good … I just did not want to stop reading." — Peter

"I think your book is amazing … I love Hannah and Rachel … Scarlett fits in perfectly." — Robyn

"Your book was the bomb.com … omg your book is amazing. I loved that ending … best book ever." — Anne

"I loved the opening paragraph of your book! It was really funny and energetic … I love your style of writing … the last sentence was great and it made me want to read more!" — Nan

"I really like your book because it reminds me of a little company that me and some of my friends have called Live Love Loom… if I told you all of them (the parts I like) this letter would be like 10 pages long … I CANNOT wait to read your second book and hopefully there will be even more." — Rachel

"I liked the ending because it leaves you on a hook ..."
— Elliot

"Please take the time to publish a second book because it is an amazing book!" — Aimee

"This book was one of the best I have ever read."
— Jenna

HANNAH SMART

Operation Josh Taylor

Melody Fitzpatrick

DUNDURN
TORONTO

Editor: Shannon Whibbs
Design: Laura Boyle
Cover Design: Courtney Horner and Laura Boyle
Cover Illustration © Evan Munday
Printer: Webcom

Library and Archives Canada Cataloguing in Publication

Fitzpatrick, Melody, author
    Operation Josh Taylor / Melody Fitzpatrick.
(Hannah Smart)

Issued in print and electronic formats.
ISBN 978-1-4597-3134-9 (pbk.).--ISBN 978-1-4597-3135-6 (pdf).-- ISBN 978-1-4597-3136-3 (epub)

    I. Title.

PS8611.I8925O64 2015   jC813'.6   C2015-900593-0
                                               C2015-900594-9

1 2 3 4 5   19 18 17 16 15

 Conseil des Arts du Canada / Canada Council for the Arts Canadä ONTARIO ARTS COUNCIL CONSEIL DES ARTS DE L'ONTARIO an Ontario government agency un organisme du gouvernement de l'Ontario

We acknowledge the support of the **Canada Council for the Arts** and the **Ontario Arts Council** for our publishing program. We also acknowledge the financial support of the **Government of Canada** through the **Canada Book Fund** and **Livres Canada Books**, and the **Government of Ontario** through the **Ontario Book Publishing Tax Credit** and the **Ontario Media Development Corporation**.

Care has been taken to trace the ownership of copyright material used in this book. The author and the publisher welcome any information enabling them to rectify any references or credits in subsequent editions.

—*J. Kirk Howard, President*

The publisher is not responsible for websites or their content unless they are owned by the publisher.

Printed and bound in Canada.

Visit us at
Dundurn.com | @dundurnpress | Facebook.com/dundurnpress | Pinterest.com/dundurnpress

Dundurn
3 Church Street, Suite 500
Toronto, Ontario, Canada
M5E 1M2

To my beautiful daughter, Erin, who is my inspiration and real-live version of Hannah Smart

1

The Josh Taylor Duh-lemma

"**H**ey, listen up all you Josh Taylor fans out there!" the radio announcer's voice blares. "It's official! Josh Taylor is *finally* going on tour and he's heading our way. He's going coast to coast and he's kicking it off right here in Glen Haven on New Year's Eve!"

O-M-G, did I hear that right? Is this true? Am I dreaming?

"That's right, fans, mark that date, because on December 31st Josh Taylor is making our very own Glen Haven, Vermont, the first stop on his cross-country tour!"

Holy crap, I'm not dreaming!

Okay, so right off the bat, I have to explain a few things:

- Number one: I love Josh Taylor. I mean *really* love him.
- Number two: I just realized that my ultimate dream is about to come true. I'm finally going to see *him* ... Josh Taylor! We'll be in the *same* room, well, actually a stadium, but who cares! We'll be literally breathing the *same air!*
- Number three: I *must* get a ticket ASAP!
- Number four: My legs have suddenly turned to Jell-O. I really have to sit down.

"Mom ... did you hear that?"

"Hear what?" she asks, whisking away at something in her bowl.

"Josh Taylor! He's coming to Glen Haven! Can you believe it?"

"No, I can't believe it." She throws in some salt.

Unbelievable! I've just told her the most exciting news — *ever* — and she can't even bother to look up. I mean, we're talking about Josh Taylor here! It's obvious that she doesn't appreciate the extreme importance of this information. I mean, imagine if the person you spent all your time dreaming of was coming to your town. Just think about it!

"Who did you say is coming?" she asks.

"Mom … Josh Taylor!" I tell her again.

"Oh, Josh Taylor." She raises an eyebrow.

"Yes, Mom, Josh Taylor. He's only the most talented singer in the entire world!"

"So I've heard," she says, rolling her eyes. "When is he coming?"

"New Year's Eve!" I shriek.

"So, I'm guessing you'll want to go to the concert, then?" she says.

"You're *guessing* I want to go to the concert?" I look at her in disbelief. "Duh!" Suddenly, I feel the sting of my hand flying against my mouth, clamping it shut before I can blurt out any other choice words.

So, let me explain. In my family, apparently, saying the word *duh* to someone is as bad as calling them a *complete idiot*, even though in my opinion, it's not even close. I found this out last week when I used the word *duh* a few too many times, and my mother, who takes things *way* too seriously, informed me that if that word passes my lips one more time there will be consequences.

"Well then, Hannah, I guess you'll have to start saving your money."

What? Excuse me?

She's showing no expression so I can't figure out if she's actually serious. So, I stare at her, waiting for her to crack. She's really not bad-looking as far as moms go. I imagine this is what I am going to look like when I get to be her age because when you look at pictures of my mom at thirteen, she looks exactly like me — average height, average weight, high cheekbones, dark brown eyes, and long dark-brown hair.

After a minute or so of staring at her, I come to the obvious conclusion that there is *no way* she can be serious. Of course she's not. She didn't like the "duh" comment and now she's trying to scare me. What a relief. I guess I'd better play along.

"I know, I know, I know." I sigh, shaking my head. "I shouldn't have said *that word*, you know … the *d-word*." I hop up on the counter beside where she's working. "I'm really, *really* sorry and I guess I'll have to accept the consequences …" I let my head fall to my chest, adding another heavy sigh for effect. I love reverse psychology! It always, always works! But something's not right. She isn't saying anything and now she's frowning.

"Mom, you can't really be serious?" I say in utter disbelief. "Save my money? What money?"

"The money you will need to buy your ticket, Hannah. Concerts are expensive, and we've been spending a lot on you lately."

What? This is crazy! This cannot be happening.

"Mom! I'm sorry I called you an idiot!"

"What?"

"I mean I'm sorry I said *duh*. I promise I'll never, ever say it again … ever!"

So, in case you haven't noticed, I am really starting to panic now. She is definitely serious!

"Oh, for heaven's sake, Hannah, stop being so dramatic. It's not about that."

"Then what's this about?" I cry.

"Just like I said, we've been spending a lot on you lately. You really need to learn the value of money. It doesn't grow on trees, you know."

I feel like saying, *Duh, what do you think, I'm a moron? Obviously, I know money doesn't grow on trees!* Still, how can she expect *me* to come up with enough money to buy my own ticket? They're expensive, you know, and I'm only thirteen, technically still a child. I mean really, what does she expect? I don't understand where this is coming from.

For the record, they haven't been spending that much money on me, and most of the stuff they bought me, I really needed. Like my new skateboard, they only bought it for me because my old one broke, and the helmet came with it, so it was free. And, now that I think about it, the skateboard should actually fall under the category of "sporting equipment," which has to do with exercise, which everyone knows is an important factor in leading an active and healthy lifestyle. They also bought me some Chuck Taylors, but only because my feet are growing and I needed sneakers. And really, how can I help it that I'm growing? I can't just look down at my feet and yell, "Stop it!" Kids grow … parents just have to deal!

Maybe she's talking about the books from Amazon. Well if she is, I don't think that's fair. Books are educational, and in my opinion, anything educational shouldn't count, should it? Even if one of them is called *A Teenager's Guide to Perfect Make-Up*, it's still a book. Right? Right! Scratch the books; they totally don't count!

So that's it really … I can't think of another thing. Well, unless she's counting the four movies I went to this month. That's only one per week, and really, I'm thinking about studying acting when I go to university someday, so I should probably go to as many movies as I can, you know, for educational purposes.

Hmmm ... she wouldn't be talking about my new iPod, would she? She totally shouldn't be. I mean, it was a back-to-school present and it was on sale! Maybe Dad told her about the new Josh Taylor album. He gave me his credit card number last week so I could download it off iTunes. Naw, I don't think she knows; she would have said something.

Right, so if I *don't* count:

- the skateboard
- the helmet
- the Chuck Taylors
- the books
- the movies
- the iPod
- and the Josh Taylor album ...

Who am I kidding? I know my mom, and she's totally counting all of it, all the stuff she knows about anyway. Crap!

"So, you're totally serious then?" I ask hopelessly.

"I am."

"So, can I ask Nan and Pops?"

"Seriously, Hannah! This is not up for debate or discussion. Begging won't help and you are not allowed to pull the 'poor old me' act with your grandparents."

"I think I need a plan," I mumble.

Mom nods. "I think you do."

2

Blame It on the Orange Crush

Okay, so I need a plan ... just one little idea. How hard can it be? I mean there's got to be a million moneymaking ideas out there. Right?

I know what you're probably thinking: why not mow a few lawns or take up babysitting? Well, for starters, mowing lawns is just out of the question — I have a huge phobia of lawnmowers ... long story, tell you later. As for babysitting, we live in a neighbourhood full of old people. There are no little kids on my street, or even close by, which I thought wouldn't be a problem, because parents want responsible and qualified babysitters, right? Wrong! After months of training, taking the highest-level babysitting course in history, and learning advanced CPR and first aid, I found out parents don't want to hire babysitters who need a ride home; they want babysitters who live across the street. How messed up is that?

So, I need to think of a plan that doesn't involve lawn mowers or taking care of small children. Usually I tap when I think. Sometimes I tap the table, sometimes I tap my desk, but right now I'm tapping my head, which by the way, is empty. I mean *really*, not a single idea, no lightning bolts of inspiration, just nothing, nada. How frustrating! Why can't I come up with just one little measly idea? Maybe I'm just not an "idea person." Hey, we can't all be geniuses. I mean, don't get me wrong, I'm no dummy, but I'm definitely not a brainiac like my friend Rachel. Now that's a girl who's super-smart, like, I'm talking … brilliant.

Rachel is my very best friend in the world and has been since the day we met, a little over five years ago. It was the first day of third grade. Rachel and I were in the same class but we didn't know each other because she was new.

So, it was lunchtime, and I was watching her (not in a *weird stalker kind of way*, but in an *I don't recognize that girl, she must be new* kind of way). Anyway, she opened her lunch bag and pulled out a strange-looking sandwich that had some weird grassy stuff in it. She took a bite and squished up her nose. Then she took out a Thermos, looked inside, and took a swig. It was pretty obvious from the look on her face that what- ever was in that Thermos was completely disgusting. I looked down at my delicious, first-day- of-school lunch that Mom packs me every year: a ham-and-cheese croissant, carrot sticks with dip, a Kit Kat bar, and a can of Orange Crush. When I looked back at Rachel, she was stuffing her lunch back into her lunch bag. I think she'd barely eaten a thing. Who could blame her, though? What kind of mother would pack a lunch like that? Then she got up from her desk and just left.

Suddenly, I found myself hopping up from my seat with my prized first day of school can of Orange Crush. *What am I doing?* I was thinking as I walked toward her empty chair. I thought about how delicious my Orange Crush would be and then about that disgusting stuff in Rachel's Thermos. I put the can down on her desk, turned to walk back to my seat, and that's when I caught him! From the corner of my eye I saw Billy Butler booking it for that can of soda. I spun around, and, as fast as lightning, bolted toward her seat. But I was too late; in the split second it took to reach Billy, he'd already grabbed it and chucked it across the room. Zach jumped up, caught it, and pitched it back. In a flash, it became a full-fledged game of Monkey in the Middle. The boys were all flailing their arms and leaping in the air, trying to catch it, while the girls were all ducking for cover. That can had to have been hurled across the classroom at least twenty times before the lunch monitor poked her head in the door and insisted that it be put away at once!

So, the game stopped; the can was put back on Rachel's desk, and everyone went back to eating lunch, including me. I didn't have my Orange Crush, but at least I had something good to eat. I checked the clock. We had fifteen minutes of lunch left. (I remember this detail because below the clock was Rachel's desk, and as my eyes fell from the clock to her, well specifically to the can of soda in her hand, I suddenly realized that she was back and nobody had filled her in; she had no idea what was about to happen.)

In my mind I was screaming, "No! No! No! New Girl ... don't do it ... don't open that can ..." But before I could warn her, she poked her finger through the loop of the pull-tab and then ... snnnnnnnnnnnap ... swishhhhhhhhhhhhh ... orange syrupy liquid was spraying everywhere, in every direction. It was all over her — in her hair, on her clothes, on her desk, on the floor. She sat frozen, like a sticky orange zombie, with everyone's eyes glued on her.

I knew one thing for sure: she needed my help. I sprang from my desk, sprinted to the craft table, and grabbed a massive roll of paper towel. Looking back now, I think everything would have been fine if I had just gone a *tiny* bit slower, but I kind of panicked.

Now to be clear, I don't think it was my fault that I slipped; the Orange Crush had turned the floor into a Slip 'N Slide, and how could I have known that Rachel would pick that exact moment to snap out of her daze and spring up from her desk?

It was like bowling a perfect strike. I hit her square on, and like a bowling pin, she went flying … and so did the can. It flew out of her hand and into the air, turning end over end, spraying an Orange Crush mist over everything in its path. When it finally landed, it was upside down on Scarlett Hastings's lap. Now, if you knew Scarlett Hastings like we know her, you would realize that this was the *worst* place for that can to land. I'll explain more about that later.

Anyway, the next thing I knew, I was waking up in the hospital with a concussion and the strangest feeling that I was being watched. Sure enough, the first thing I saw, as soon as I was able to focus, were two big blue eyes staring at me through a tangled mess of sticky, long, strawberry-blond hair. Those eyes, peering at me from the next bed over, belonged to Rachel. She was also the proud owner of ten brand new stitches, a broken arm, and a new best friend.

In the hospital we found out how much we had in common. Most importantly, this is where we discovered we were (and still are) Josh Taylor's absolute biggest fans!

Wait a second … *we* are his biggest fans … *Rachel and me* … could it be that easy? Of course it is. I just figured out a plan, a brilliant plan. I'll call Rachel! She'll know exactly what to do. Problem solved! I told you I'm no dummy.

3

The Highs and Lows of Celebration Pizza

"Hey, Mrs. Carter, is Rachel around?" I say into the phone.

"Well, she is supposed to be in her room doing her homework, but you know Rachel."

So, I told you Rachel is smart, but the weird thing is she hates pretty much everything to do with school, especially homework. Her mom is always on her case about this. I guess it makes sense though since her mom is a teacher, well actually a university professor. She teaches holistic nutrition, which, according to Rachel, just means she teaches people how to be completely obsessed with organic food. Rachel's dad is a pediatric surgeon. So, it's not surprising that Rachel's IQ is like over 140, not that she seems to care. This is the one thing I don't get about Rachel. I'd love to be smart like that. I know it drives them crazy when she goofs off, which *I hope* she's not doing now, but *I know* she probably is.

"Rachel Lynn Carter!" I hear her mom bellow. "Turn the music down! What are you doing?"

I hear Rachel mumble something in the background. She's probably doing a Josh portrait again. She's super talented, and she should be; she gets *lots* of practice. I think every girl in our class has at least one of her Josh Taylor sketches.

"What's up?" she says, with a sigh.

I can tell by her voice that I was right; she's in trouble *again,* but right now I've got *much* more important things on my mind.

"You are not going to believe what I am about to tell you!" I squeal.

"What?"

"It's the best news!"

"What!"

"Oh, you are going to be *so* excited!"

"What is it?"

"Well, how would you like to see …"

"Wait …" she cuts me off in midsentence. "My mother is *freaking*! I have to go. Call you later."

Then there's a click and a dial tone.

This is beyond terrible on so many levels. I didn't get to tell her about Josh, and she didn't get to help me with my plan!

Suddenly, as if by magic, the phone rings. Thank god!

"Hey!" I say anxiously. "Wow, that was fast! So, like I was saying, how would you like to see …"

"Hannah, what are you talking about?"

"Oh, Dad … it's you."

"You were expecting someone else?"

"Yeah, Rachel."

"Well, never mind about that now," he says. "Tell your mom I'm bringing home pizza and I've got some exciting news."

Hmmm … pizza … exciting news? What a coincidence! We both have exciting news today. Unless his exciting news and my exciting news are the same exciting news! It must be! I mean what else could it be? I bet Mom felt bad and called him, or maybe he heard it on the radio. Well, one thing is for sure, he wants to surprise me and he's bringing home pizza to celebrate! My dad is so cool!

"Tell me now! I can't wait until you get home," I squeal.

"You're just going to have to wait, but it will be worth it. I promise!" I can hear the smile in his voice.

Well, that's proof enough for me; Josh Taylor here I come!

I'm going crazy waiting for Rachel to call, which hopefully will be soon. I mean this is way too exciting to keep to myself!

About fifteen minutes later, Dad arrives home with our "celebration pizza."

"Hi, honey," he says, smiling as he puts the box down on the counter.

"Hi, Dad. I can't wait to hear your news!" I say, beaming. His smile gets even wider and he throws me a wink. A wink! You know what that means …

At the table, even though I'm sure I know what's coming, I'm still sitting on pins and needles, barely tasting my supper, waiting to hear those words: *Sweet Hannah, we're taking you to the Josh Taylor concert!*

And then I'll say (for Mom's benefit), *But Dad, I can't go to the concert. I have no money to buy a ticket.*

Then Dad will say, *Oh darling, you don't need money. We want to take you because we know you are Josh Taylor's biggest fan!*

And then I'll look into my mother's eyes and she'll see how happy I am, and she'll look into my father's eyes and see how happy he is, and then she'll reach across the table and take our hands in hers, smile, and say, *Okay you can go to the concert and we will totally pay.*

"Hannah, lift up your glass, your dad is making a toast!" Mom frowns.

"What … now?" I stammer. Oh, here it comes! I can hardly wait! Okay, pretend to look surprised.

I lift my glass of Coke and Dad starts, "Today I learned some very exciting news. I think you're going to be very …"

Just then the phone rings. Mom gets up.

"Hannah, it's Rachel." She gestures for me to make it quick.

"Hi," Rachel whispers, "tell me what's going on, but do it fast 'cause if Mom catches me on the phone, I'm dead."

"Hi," I say quickly, "I can't talk now because we're eating supper! I'll call you back later!" I slam down the phone and rush back to my seat at the table. "Okay, Dad, as you were saying?"

"Okay," he says, raising his eyebrow. "This afternoon I got some wonderful news. Actually, it's great news for all of us! I just found out I'm getting a big promotion at work."

"But Dad, I can't go to the concert. I have no money to buy a ticket," I say with a sigh.

Dad shakes his head. "Hannah, what are you talking about?"

"You just said you were taking us to the Josh Taylor concert, and I said I don't have money for a ticket." I glance over at my mom, who is frowning.

"I didn't say anything about a concert." He looks confused.

"You didn't? I'm sure you just said you were taking us to the concert. Didn't you?"

"No, Hannah, I said I got a big promotion at work."

"Promotion?" I repeat dumbly.

"Yes, promotion! This is my exciting news! This is what I've been trying to tell you!" His face is beaming. "Today I got a promotion."

You know when you're in a soccer game and you're right beside the net, the ball is speeding toward you, and you've got a clear shot to score the winning goal, but instead the ball slams you right in the gut …

No one seems to notice that I'm in a state of shock. Why would they care? They have *exciting news* to talk about. What's so exciting about a stupid promotion anyway? I mean a promotion is just … well, a better job and more money and … wait a second … I think I may have possibly found a silver lining to this grey cloud of information.

"Hey, Dad," I say, flashing a big smile, "congratulations on your promotion. So I guess that means you're going to be making, like, tons of more money, right?"

He smiles back. "Well Hannah, it means a lot of things, and yes, a nice boost to my salary is one of them. It also means that there's going to be a few changes around here. I'll be working a lot and so I won't be home as much as I am now. Your mother is going to need you to help out more." He reaches over to give my mom's hand a squeeze. For some reason she isn't smiling back. Weird … you'd think she'd be crazy happy about a nice fat paycheque! Instead, she gets up and starts clearing the table.

"So, Dad," I say in my sweetest voice, "I heard some exciting news today, too. Josh Taylor is coming to Glen Haven. Isn't that exciting?"

"I'm sure it is for you, Hannah," he says.

"Yeah, so I *really* want to go to his concert," I blurt out.

"That's nice," he replies, totally not taking the bait.

"Well, Dad, with your new raise and everything, do you think you'd have enough money to buy me a ticket?" I half whisper.

"Yeah, I think I could manage that," he whispers back, smiling.

"Really! You could manage it?" I say in a hushed squeal.

He nods. "Yup, I think I can definitely manage it."

Wow, that was easy! He said yes! It's totally official! I am going to see Josh Taylor, live in concert, breathing the same air and …

"Manage what?" says my mother from across the kitchen.

I shove a piece of pizza in my mouth.

"Hannah just asked me …" Dad starts.

"Mmmmm," I say loudly, with my mouth full, "this pizza is *so* good!"

My mother's eyes narrow. "Hannah, what did you ask your father?"

"Oh, Mom," I scold her, "this is Dad's night, not mine. Let's not talk about me."

"Hannah, I know what's going on here," she says, frowning, "and it's not going to happen."

Great, and just like that another soccer ball slams me right in the gut.

My stomach hurts.

4

Two Plans Are Better Than One

When I arrive at school the next morning, the volume level is louder than usual, especially with the girls; every one of them is wearing an ear-to-ear grin as they chatter away in their little groups. One of them is holding a newspaper. She points to something on the front page, lets out a little squeal, and then clutches it to her heart.

I need to find Rachel!

I scan the hallway. I peek in her classroom for the third time, and then check the hallway again. I'm desperate to find her. When I called her back last night she was still banned from the phone and the Internet. She probably doesn't even know yet!

I spot her just as the bell rings. She's actually sticking out like a sore thumb because she appears to be the only girl in the whole school who is frowning. Actually, this is great! She can't possibly know. I'll get to tell her myself!

I run in her direction, ignoring the bell.

"So, Josh Taylor," I say breathlessly.

"Yeah I know," she replies.

"You know?"

Hmmm … honestly, at this point, I am a smidge worried. I mean Josh Taylor is coming! Why is she not jumping for joy over this monumentally amazing news?

"Yeah, your mom called my mom last night."

"She did?" I gulp.

"Yup, she did." Rachel purses her lips.

"What did she say?"

"Well, she told my mom about the concert." She puts her finger to her chin. "Oh, and she might have also mentioned something about us *buying our own our own tickets*, and how it would be a great opportunity to *teach us some responsibility*."

"Responsibility?" I say closing my eyes. "Oh no, don't tell me …"

"Yeah," she blurts out, "I have to buy my own ticket, too."

"Sorry," I say, secretly relieved that we're both in the same boat. "My mother … you *know* how she is. Sometimes she can be so … motherly."

"That's okay," Rachel says, hunching her shoulders. "We'll figure something out."

Suddenly, we hear the familiar cackle of Scarlett Hastings. She's coming down the hall with Anika and Missy, who are her "yes-girls." They trail behind her everywhere she goes and agree with everything she says. She pushes them around constantly, but they never seem to notice.

Strutting towards us, the three of them look like they're auditioning for *America's Next Top Model*.

"The bell rang you know," Scarlett snarls, flicking her long, glistening, black hair over her shoulder. On cue, Anika and Missy follow suit with the stupid hair flick. As usual, they are on either side of Scarlett; they look like a couple of hair-flicking bookends.

"After school. My house. Planning session," Rachel says with a quick nod, as she turns toward her classroom.

"Planning session? Ewwww, sounds serious!" Scarlett says, rolling her eyes. "Spill," she demands, flashing the fakest smile ever.

We both know better than to tell Scarlett anything, especially this.

"It's none of your business Scarlett," Rachel replies.

"None of my business?" Scarlett raises an eyebrow. "As if I actually care," she huffs.

"Well you asked," I say under my breath.

"Whatever the two of you are up to, I'm sure it's …" she pauses a second and narrows her eyes, "um … totally lame."

"Lame," Anika adds with a nod.

"Yeah, totally," Missy adds, looking confused.

"Well, it's been fun, Scarlett, but we have to get back to class," I say.

"Whatever …" Scarlett yawns, walking away, motioning for the bookends to follow.

* * *

After school we head over to Rachel's house to devise our plan.

"Hey, would you girls like a snack?" her mom asks as we come in the kitchen. "I just got back from the grocery store so there are lots of goodies in the fridge." She points to their massive refrigerator.

"Goodies?" I whisper to Rachel.

"They're *goodies* to her," she whispers back, grimacing.

So, we fix ourselves a snack of fat-free, organic brown rice cakes smothered in 100 percent natural, unsweetened, sodium-reduced, organic peanut butter. Then we pour ourselves two tall glasses of low-fat, organic chocolate soy milk — all of this as close to junk food as Rachel's mom will probably ever get.

Upstairs in her room, Rachel has a big easel with a roll of paper attached. She tears off her most recent Josh Taylor original, and pulls down the torn edge of the paper to reveal a clean, new page. She takes the cap off a purple Sharpie and writes OPERATION JOSH TAYLOR across the top.

"What do you think?" she asks.

"Perfect!" I say, beaming. I can't believe how easy this is going to be! I mean it's only been like a minute and we already have the perfect name for our plan. This is going to be a breeze!

Rachel turns on her radio. "What next?"

"What next?" I ask, confused.

"Any ideas?"

"Well, my idea was to call you. Now it's your turn."

"Well, I thought of the name!" she says.

"Okay, but, hello … I tried to come up with a plan already and the only one I could think of was to call you."

"Well, what about a hunger strike?" she says, jokingly.

"Are you serious … a hunger strike? Do you even know me at all?" I ask, shoving the last bite of peanut-butter-smeared rice cake into my mouth.

"Oh yeah," Rachel replies. "Hey, what about grandparents?"

"Nope, already warned not to go there."

"I know — we could start a lawn-mowing service!" she says, pushing an imaginary lawn mower around her room.

"Lawn-mowing?" I look at her in horror. I can't believe that she, of all people, could even consider such a thing. She knows the last time I tried to mow a lawn was a disaster!

Let me explain. Earlier this month, after probably an hour's worth of very lengthy safety instructions on how to properly operate a lawn mower, my dad finally let me try it out. I started the mower perfectly, and went on to mow a nice straight line. I must say, I was pretty proud of myself. All that changed, though, when Rachel's mom drove by and Rachel stuck her head out of the car window. I just let go of the mower for a split second to wave to her when the thing went crazy and took off across the lawn, kind of zigzagging right toward my mother's brand-new car. I tore off across the yard after it like a maniac. Lunging forward, I almost had it in my grasp when suddenly I felt my foot roll over my soccer ball. As I flew through the air, it felt like everything was going in slow motion. Then, with a sudden smack, I landed face-first into my mother's flower garden, which was planted along the edge of the driveway. As I pried my face from the dirt, the sound of the slicing mower blades and the roaring motor became almost deafening. I whipped my head around, horrified, to see  that out-of-control-beast-of-a-mower heading straight for me. If you ever had a moment when you saw your life flashing before your eyes, I'm sure you can relate, because, this was my moment. Suddenly, I felt two arms locking under mine, pulling me out of the flower patch. Just as I managed to twist my head around to see that it was Rachel who was rescuing me from certain death, the sound of high-pitched, ear-splitting screams drew my attention back to the garden, and to my mother, who, at that very moment, had returned home from her run just in time to see the charging-beast-of-a-mower, which was obviously possessed, smash viciously into her brand-new, gleaming, candy-apple-red Toyota Prius.

So to recap, the last time I attempted to use a lawn mower I:

1. Mowed down a freshly planted flower garden,
2. Caused $750.00 damage to my mother's new car,
3. Nearly got killed, and
4. Lost all electronics for two weeks, including the computer, the TV, my Xbox, and my brand-new iPod.

So, I'm sure you can understand why I can't believe that Rachel, who witnessed this entire horrific event, could even say the word *lawn mower* in my presence, let alone suggest that we start a lawn-mowing service!

"Oh, yeah …" she says, biting her lip, "Sorry … how could I forget?"

"A lawn-mowing service, I mean, seriously?" I roll my eyes.

"I think we need some fresh air," Rachel says, looking out the window. "Hey, Mom is teaching a yoga class in the backyard. Maybe we should join in. Might help us clear our minds."

I look out the window at all the ladies dressed in their lululemon yoga gear, all perfectly positioned in neat rows, doing their best attempts at downward-facing dog. I have a lululemon hoodie, which I totally love. I got it at a yard sale last September for five bucks. What a deal!

"Hannah, listen!" Rachel demands, pointing at her radio. "Turn it up!"

"That's right!" the announcer booms. *"I'm looking at a big pile of front-row tickets to see Josh Taylor live in concert! Every day from now until December we'll be giving them away. Just listen for Josh's latest number one hit, 'Heart Attack.' When you hear it, start dialling. The tenth caller on the line who can correctly answer the daily Josh Taylor trivia question will win two front-row tickets to see Josh live in concert right here in Glen Haven! So fans, start brushing up on your Josh trivia!"*

"Josh trivia! We know Josh trivia. We know everything about Josh Taylor!" I squeal.

"We do, we're his biggest fans!" Rachel adds excitedly.

"Yeah, we don't need a plan! We can win the tickets!" I yell, jumping in the air.

"Operation Win Tickets!" she yells back, jumping beside me.

Just then, Rachel's older brother, Nate, pokes his head in the door.

"Hey losers!" he says, in his surfer-dude accent. "Wanna turn that down?"

"Wanna get out of my room?" Rachel yells above the blaring radio that's now playing our newest favorite Josh Taylor song, "Lovin' You."

"What's with you two, anyway?" He smirks.

"We're gonna win tickets to the Josh Taylor concert," I say, matter-of-factly.

"You think you're going to win tickets?" He raises his eyebrow. "You mean from that radio contest?"

"Well, yeah," Rachel barks, "we are! Definitely! Well, probably, er … hopefully!"

Rachel's brother shakes his head. "You realize there's like hundreds, maybe thousands, of teen-age girls trying to get those tickets. Right?"

"Hundreds … maybe thousands?" I gasp.

Nate chuckles. "Yeah, you're *not* gettin' tickets."

"Thanks for your help, *Nate*. Now get out of my room!" Rachel demands, chucking her pillow at him.

Reality check: Nate is right. The chances of us actually winning tickets are pretty slim.

Looking out the window again, I see that all the yoga ladies are now on their tiptoes with their arms stretching up to the clouds. It looks like they bought out the entire lululemon store. For a second, I forget all about the plan and let thoughts of my own lovely lululemon sweater float around in my brain. It was so sweet finding it on that table in my neighbour's driveway. And the look on Scarlett's face when she saw me wearing it at school the next day was, like, priceless. She thought she was the only kid in our school with lulu stuff. Ha! I'm so glad I went to that sale!

Suddenly it's staring me right in the face … the perfect plan.

"Rachel!" I exclaim. "We're gonna have a yard sale."

5

Operation-a-No-Go

I've been telling Rachel all week not to worry so much. It's all going to work out. Actually, I'm so sure of it that I've already picked out an outfit for the concert, and it's still months away! After all, we not only have a plan, Operation Yard Sale, but with our combined *expert knowledge* of all things Josh Taylor, we have a great backup plan. Not that we'll need a backup plan because our yard sale is going to be massive! A monster blowout! We just need to find some stuff to sell.

Since last week, we've been searching through our rooms for old clothes and "gently used" junk. Rachel thinks we don't have enough. Even with all of Rachel's obsessing, I'm not going to freak about it. I'm sure we'll find enough stuff to sell by Saturday. We've got loads of time. Although, it's turning out to be a bit tougher than I thought. It seems sometimes, it's a teensy-weensy bit difficult to practically give away a once-prized possession for, like, an eighth of what it's worth. For example, I have this really awesome, fleecy, light-blue Hollister hoodie. It's cozy and warm and I love it. So, okay, the arms are just a tiny bit short and the zipper gets stuck sometimes, and it kind of rides up whenever I sit down. I am really trying to force myself to throw it onto the sell-it pile, but I love it so much. And it's been such an important part of my life. I've worn it to many events and on lots and lots of special occasions, although I can't exactly remember which ones at this moment in time. Anyway, it's one of my favorite things I own, so how could I possibly sell it? Of course I can't. I'll just remember not to lift up my arms or sit down when I'm wearing it. Great! It's decided then: I am not selling it!

So, this is pretty much how things have gone all week. Our sell-it piles are pathetically small and our rooms are disasters.

Finally, Rachel suggests we work on our piles together.

"So," she says, "I think we should start using a 'tough love approach.'"

"Tough love?" I stare at her, eyebrows raised, thinking that this should be interesting.

"So, say I'm having a particularly hard time letting go of something I *really* love," she says, "like say … a big stack of old *J-14* magazines."

"Or a cozy hoodie," I say under my breath.

"So, now it's your job to be *tough* and say something like, *I know you love them, but you've read them a trillion times and took out all the cool posters and now they're all falling apart.*

Then, we'll take the whole bunch and put them in the sell-it pile!" She puts her hands on her hips and smiles. "Get it? Tough … love!"

"I get it. Tough … love. What a great idea …"

I frown, suddenly eyeing *her* eyeing *my* hoodie lying on the bed.

"So, let's start with that sweater of yours!" she says, reaching down to take it.

"Absolutely not!" I scowl, whipping it off the bed just in the nick of time. "Not my warm, cozy, special-occasion Hollister hoodie!"

"Special-occasion hoodie? How is that a 'special-occasion hoodie'?" she asks.

Hmmm … out of all the reasons I just listed for why this sweater should absolutely not be included in the sell-it pile, she had to pick that one! Figures.

"Well … well …" I hesitate. "It was a special occasion when I bought it."

"Hannah …" Rachel reaches to take it from me.

"No way!" I yell, tightening my grip.

"It's too small for you!" She tugs at it.

"No, it is not!" I protest, tugging back.

"Yes, it is, Hannah," she says, tightening her grip.

"No, it's not!" I say, giving my hoodie a good yank.

"Hannah, the cuffs don't even cover your wrists anymore."

"Only when I lift up my arms or stretch or something."

"Give it to me!" She yanks at it again.

"No, Rachel, please find something else," I plead in desperation.

"Come on, you can do it," she prods.

"No, I can't," I stammer.

"Yes, you can. Tough love, remember?"

"You really think it's too small?"

"Yes, Hannah. It's definitely too small."

My fingers are stiff and getting sore and my knuckles are turning white.

"Are you sure? I mean they could totally be like three-quarter-length sleeves, you know."

"They're not three-quarter length sleeves. It's TOO SMALL, HANNAH."

"Really?"

"Yes!"

"Okay, fine. I give up." I know she's right. We'll have to use this stupid "tough love" rule or we'll never find anything to sell.

"Hannah."

"What?"

"You have to let go of it." Rachel frowns.

"Oh yeah, sorry," I stammer as I uncurl my

fingers. "Take it quick before I change my mind." I turn my head so I don't have to see her toss it on the pile.

"Now, that wasn't too hard," she says smiling.

"Yes, it was." I flex my sore fingers, look over at the pile, and sigh.

"What next?" She rubs her palms together as she scans my room for more loot.

* * *

For the rest of the week we practise Rachel's "tough love" method to sort our junk and it turns out there is a lot of it. I can  hardly believe that tomorrow is the big day: Operation Yard Sale. We're super pumped and ready to sell. Good thing, too, because up to this point the only thing Operation Win Tickets has produced is frustration.

We've been calling into the station every day since the beginning of the contest and we haven't gotten through, even once! This is extra crappy because every time we called, we had the right answer. I'm not going to let it get me down though, because tomorrow is going to be a *great* day and our yard sale is going to be a major success! I can feel it in my bones!

* * *

BEEP! BEEP! BEEP! BEEP! BEEP! Bang! It's 5:45 a.m. and I think I may have smashed my alarm clock. Oh well, at least I made it stop. I roll over and shake Rachel. "Get up," I whisper. She's not moving an inch.

"Rachel, it's time to get up," I say a little louder this time. Still nothing. I'm pretty sure she's not dead; she's just not a morning person. But this morning of all mornings she needs to move!

"RACHEL LYNN CARTER!" I yell.

She pries open one eye. "Mom?" she whispers.

"No, you loser! It's Hannah. It's time for our yard sale!"

She pries open the other eye and kind of stares right through me and then closes them both. Then she does the unthinkable — she rolls over and starts to snore. Unbelievable!

This won't do! I grab her by the ankles and start pulling her out of bed. As she kicks me away from her, I remember just how much she values her sleep. So there she is, half hanging out of my bed, sound asleep. I have no choice but to finish the job, so with one swift pull of her feet, she is on the floor, moaning. At least she's awake.

"What's that sound?" she says with her eyes still clamped shut.

"What sound?"

"I think I hear rain," she growls.

Just then a branch smacks against the window with a loud crack.

I rush to the window to confirm Operation Yard Sale is a complete washout.

6

Vegetarians Don't Eat Chicken

So, here we are 6:00 a.m., Saturday morning with nothing to do but listen to rain, which is coming down in buckets. The wind is howling, and the lights in my bedroom just flickered. According to the guy on the radio, we're in the middle of a tropical storm. No wonder the windows are rattling.

Rachel shrugs. "Too bad we couldn't have had the yard sale last week when it was warm and sunny."

"Guess we should have checked the weather forecast."

"Yeah." Rachel frowns. "Your dad *is* a meteorologist."

"Well, maybe I could have asked him if he were ever home," I say throwing up my arms in frustration. "He's always working now, and when he is home, he's tired and grouchy. You know what? His new job kinda sucks."

"Yeah, your mom said the same thing when she was over for yoga the other day. Anyway, let's remember to check the forecast next time, okay?"

"So, I wonder what else we forgot?"

Rachel throws her arms up. "Advertising! We forgot advertising." She looks out the window. "We didn't put an ad in the paper; we didn't even put up a single poster."

"You know," I say, looking out the window at my waterlogged neighbourhood, "maybe this rain did us a favour. Now we have an extra week to make it even better!"

"Yeah, I guess at least we have time to do some promotion."

"Rachel, we can do better than that!" I exclaim. "Look at all those driveways." I point out the window.

"Okay, what are you getting at?" She lowers her eyebrows.

"What about a huge sale with the entire neighbourhood! Don't you think it would bring in, like, way more people than a single yard sale? Plus, we can split the cost of advertising with all the neighbours!"

"Hannah Smart!" Rachel says, grinning. "You are living up to your name."

* * *

For the rest of the week we knock on doors, rallying the neighbourhood for our new and improved plan: Operation Street Sale. We put an ad in the paper, make posters, and even plan a coffee-and-muffin station.

The week flies by and before we know it, Saturday morning arrives. The sky is clear and forecast is super. Everything is perfect.

"Okay, here we go!" Rachel squeals, and pinches my arm as she spies an old couple approaching the driveway.

"I'm already picturing those concert tickets in my hand," I whisper.

"Nice morning girls," the old guy says, as he scans the driveway.

"Oh, look, Harold!" the lady exclaims. "The girls are selling bran muffins." She claps her hands together. "I love bran muffins! How much are your bran muffins dear?"

"I'm sorry," Rachel, says, "but we only have chocolate chip. Would you like one?"

"I'd like a bran muffin, please," the lady replies, smiling.

"I'm sorry. We don't have bran muffins," Rachel says, slowly.

"Well, yes you do, dear." The old lady grins, shaking her head. "They're right there."

"They're chocolate chip," I repeat, trying to save Rachel.

"But I don't like chocolate chip!" she cries. "I like bran muffins."

"These are really delicious, even better than bran muffins!" I say, nodding.

"I'm sure they are dear. Now how much are your bran muffins?"

"Um …" I start.

"We're looking for china," her husband cuts in.

"Royal Albert, Old Country Roses," the lady says smiling. "Such a lovely pattern. Please show me your china dear."

"No, sorry. We only have …"

"Ooooo-wee. Lookie there, old girl!" the old guy interrupts me, pointing to my neighbour Gertrude's driveway. "Looks like a good one over there!"

"Oh my!" The lady's eyes widen as she spies Gertrude's driveway overflowing with yard-sale treasures. "I hope they have bran muffins."

My neighbour Gertrude is, like, seventy-eight years old, and downsizing: she's moving into a condo or nursing home or something. Anyway, her whole front lawn and driveway are littered with old furniture and dishes and crap, so she'll probably have something they'll want. Who knows, she might even have bran muffins.

The next couple wanders in munching on granola bars and sipping from their eco-friendly water bottles.

This time I am *determined* to sell something.

"Would you have anything baby-related?" the guy asks, searching the driveway.

"I'm expecting … my first," the woman says, beaming, as she rubs her hand over her giant belly.

"No, sorry. No baby stuff," Rachel replies, squishing up her nose.

"Well, could we interest you in some coffee or a freshly baked muffin?" I ask.

They both hold up their water bottles. "No thanks. We're good."

"Okay, then," I say, scrambling to pick up a book from the table, "could I interest you in this great cookbook? *101 Ways to Cook a Chicken*!" I hold it up to show her. "It's got loads of great recipes, and it even has a very informative section on how to take all the bones out! See …" I flip the cookbook open to the "Deboning a Chicken Carcass" page and point to a picture at the top where a lady is stabbing a sharp knife into a raw chicken.

"First, lift the skin of the chicken's neck with a sharp blade," I read from the book, "then, saw the wishbone from the chicken's flesh and give it a good yank. Drive your knife in deeply to separate the bones from the soft, fleshy tissue. Then slice the connections of the legs and the wings to the carcass. Pull the leg toward you so the thigh bone pops completely out of its socket." I look up at her with my widest smile and try to pass her the book.

Her eyes are bulging out of her head. "No, I don't want it!" she cries, thrusting the book back at me.

Wow, I was not expecting that reaction. I mean, I gave a pretty impressive sales pitch. Actually, if my mom hadn't given us this book to sell, I'd seriously think about buying it for her myself!

"We don't eat chicken," the pregnant woman says in complete disgust. She's actually starting to gag a bit.

"Really?" I say confused. "But chicken is such a healthy choice for your family. Maybe you should consider it." I pat her belly. "It's low-fat!"

"I'm not fat!" she protests angrily, "I'm pregnant!"

"I wasn't calling you fat," I stammer, "I just meant …"

"Listen, kid!" she cuts me off. "We're vegetarians! Not depraved chicken butchers!"

"So, are you sure?" I shrug. "I mean, think of the baby. Everyone needs protein, especially that poor little innocent infant growing in there." I point to her belly.

"Yes, I'm sure!" she yells, quickly waddling away.

"Well, think about it!" I shout, holding up the book as I scurry after her.

She glances back and for a second, I think she might be changing her mind, but then suddenly, a look of terror appears on her face. *Is she afraid of me?* She starts speeding up, almost running, kind of like a crazy duck, wibble-wobbling toward the street.

"Stay away from me you ... you ... CRAZY-CHICKEN-MURDERING-CARNIVORE!"

That's when something completely awful happens; I trip over my shoelace and accidentally lose my grip on *101 Ways to Murder a Chicken*. As it's flying through the air, Mrs. Definitely-Not-Fat-Just-Pregnant-Vegetarian-Lady catches sight of it, and, thank god, ducks down out of its path. It flies straight over her head and lands with a loud smack on the pavement in front of her.

Her husband shoots me a disgusted glare, puts his arm around his poor, traumatized wife, and leads her wibble-wobbling across the street to Gertrude's driveway.

At that moment, a car door slams and we look up to see a lady and her daughter getting out of a big black SUV. I have a feeling that our luck is about to change. But sadly, that feeling only lasts a second. Suddenly, we realize we're looking at Scarlett Hastings and her mother. The Hastings family lives in a huge house a few streets over. Scarlett's mom is tall and slim with shiny, jet-black hair that's always *perfectly* done. She's a fashion buyer, so she's always dressed up in something designer. Scarlett is like a mini version of her mom; her satiny black hair is pulled back into a perfectly neat ponytail and she's wearing brand-name everything from head to toe. It's easy to feel plain next to Scarlett Hastings.

"Okay, we can do this," Rachel whispers to me through a forced smile.

"Hi Scarlett," I say.

"Could we interest you in a coffee or a chocolate-chip muffin?" Rachel points to our snack station.

Scarlett's mother glances at our muffin display, rolls her eyes, and then shakes her head no.

"Do you realize how many grams of fat are in those muffins?" Scarlett sneers.

"They're low-fat," Rachel exclaims. "It said so on the package!"

"They're from a package?" Scarlett throws her head back, laughing. "How pedestrian!"

"Pe-dest-what?" I frown.

"Low-class," Rachel whispers quickly.

"Low-class?" I grit my teeth.

Scarlett's mother raises her eyebrow at Rachel, takes one sweeping glance at our stuff, and then walks away, leaving Scarlett behind with us.

"Can I help you find something, Scarlett?" I ask.

"Find something here? You've *got* to be kidding," she scoffs, picking up my Hollister hoodie.

"Well, why are you here, then?" I frown. "I mean, isn't this a little too pedestrian for you?"

"Yeah, you're right, it is. Actually, we're looking for antique furniture for the summer house."

"Antique furniture? Try over there," Rachel makes a face, pointing toward Gertrude's place.

"Oh, that's where everybody is," Scarlett chirps with a smirk. "Good luck selling any of this junk." She walks away laughing, tossing my once-prized hoodie over her shoulder and onto the grass. How freaking rude!

After Scarlett makes her exit, the morning turns around, and we start selling like crazy. It's like people are almost throwing money at us. And what a wonderful feeling it is to see kids all over the neighbourhood holding our balloons and eating our Jumbo Freezies.

At 1:00 we decide to pack up. Since I've been handling the money end of things, I count up the profits while Rachel loads up my dad's car with the leftover stuff for Goodwill.

"How much did we make?" Rachel squeals, excitedly.

I smile. "Well, the good news is we made a profit."

"Rachel's face falls, "The good news? What's the bad news?"

"We didn't make as much money as I thought."

"Yes, we did!" Rachel argues. "We made tons of money. We made enough for the tickets, right?"

"Not exactly."

"What do you mean, not exactly? How much did we make?"

"Ten bucks."

"How could we have only made ten bucks?" Rachel cries. "We sold tons of stuff; I even sold some of my artwork!"

"Well, maybe our expenses were too high."

"Our expenses!" Rachel exclaims. "Hannah, you said you were good at handling money! How much were our expenses? How much was the ad in the paper?"

"Well, the ad was cheap because I split the cost with the neighbourhood," I say, "and Gertrude lent me the money for our supplies. Wasn't that nice of her?" I smile hopefully.

"Super," Rachel answers sarcastically. "How much were the balloons?"

"Only a dollar-fifty each."

"One-fifty each!" she yells.

"They were filled with helium!"

"Well, how much did you sell them for?"

"How much did I sell them for?" I frown.

"They were freebies. I gave them away!"

"How many, Hannah?"

"Only thirty."

"Oh, Hannah ..." Rachel lets out a deep sigh. "Please tell me you charged for all of those Jumbo Freezies."

I look down at the ground.

"Hannah!"

"Well, the balloons and the Freezies brought in a lot of business! So did the samples!" I add.

"The samples?" Rachel asks slowly.

"Yeah, well, the muffins weren't selling so well, so I cut some up for a little *try before you buy*. Seemed like a good idea at the time."

"I thought we sold all those muffins." Rachel frowns.

"Well, we sold a few and I ate a few, and the rest I gave away."

"Oh, Hannah ..." She closes her eyes and sighs again.

"Sorry," I say, wiping a crumb from my mouth.

"What now?" Rachel shakes her head.

"We try again."

"Another yard sale?" She looks horrified.

"Of course not!" I sneer.

Rachel throws her arms up. "Then what? What are we going to do?"

"People *want* to spend money, Rachel. We just have to figure out *what* they want to spend it on."

"Yeah, that's the challenging part, especially since we have nothing left to sell."

"Well, it's a good thing we like challenges," I say.

7

V.I.P. Also Stands for Vile Inconsiderate (or Icky) Person

With the yard sale over, the rest of the weekend was dedicated to homework, which was fine with me because I had an assignment to finish, an assignment on Josh Taylor (I know … big surprise!). In my defence, I had to write about a topic I felt deeply connected to. So, you can see I really didn't have much choice. Josh Taylor was perfect subject material!

My project is due today, and it's an oral presentation, so I'll be speaking in front of the class. A lot of people get totally freaked out by public speaking, but not me. I like being in front of a crowd. It makes me feel kind of important, like I'm a teacher or an actor or something. I'm actually a little excited about today, especially since I'll be "teaching" every-one about Josh Taylor!

Yesterday I spent hours doing research, verify-ing facts, and checking out all the latest Josh Taylor gossip on *celebritydish.com*. This is where I found out that Josh was seen only last week hav-ing lunch with some mystery woman at the Manhattan Grill and Oyster Bar in New York City, and then later that same day, he was seen again at a New York hospital with the same woman when she was taken by ambu-lance to the emergency department. Cool, huh?

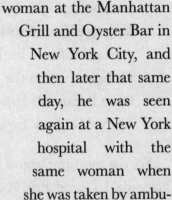

Once my research was done, I went on *you-can-do-anything.com* to get some pointers on how to give an *exciting* and *effective* presentation.

This is what I found out:

1. **Know Your Material and Practise**: No problem! My material, I know inside and out, backwards and forwards, and

practice; who needs practice when you *so* know your material? Just the same, I ran over everything with Rachel on the phone last night.

2. **Overcome Nervousness**: Totally not a problem, but if I was nervous, I would just picture all the guys in my class wearing hot-pink bras. (Try it sometime; it really works!)

3. **Engage Your Audience:** I'm planning to start off with a joke. If I get them laughing, I'll have them in the *palm of my hand!*

4. **Stay Focused:** How hard can it be to stay focused on Josh Taylor? Piece of cake!

So, the morning begins with a presentation on Formula 1 Grand Prix Racing. Surprisingly, it's way more interesting than I expected. The next presentation is on *Dance Dance Revolution*, and as it turns out, is way less interesting than I expected.

"Okay Hannah, you're next," Mrs. Walker says, looking at her watch.

I look out at the rows of the bored faces and smile.

"Good morning everyone!" I say, a little louder than I'd planned. "I'm so happy to be here today." Out of the corner of my eye I can see Scarlett passing a note to Billy Butler. He reads it and nods, letting out a snort of laughter.

 I know it's best to ignore them; hopefully it has nothing to do with me. But just the same, Billy Butler, at least in my mind, is now wearing a lovely, hot-pink, polka-dot bra with matching underwear.

"So, a doctor, a lawyer, two hillbillies, and a priest walk into a bar. The doctor says —"

"Hannah, is this a joke?" Mrs. Walker interrupts me. She really has a scowl on. She obviously has no sense of humour at all! I mean, who doesn't like a joke?

"It's part of my presentation," I reply honestly. "I'm trying to engage my audience."

"Hannah, just stick to the facts."

"But —"

"Hannah, please get on with it."

"But, I need to engage —"

"Hannah! The facts only, please!"

"Okay," I reluctantly agree. "So, as I was saying, I'm super excited to be here today to talk to you about someone I truly admire, someone with massive talent, someone with enormous determination, and someone who is, like, super, majorly hot ..." I glance over at Mrs. Walker and see she's pursing her lips. "I mean ... um ... very good-looking."

"Go on, Hannah," Mrs. Walker prods, motioning with her hand.

"So, let me start by asking how many of you know who Josh Taylor is?"

All the girls' hands immediately shoot into the air.

"Great, so now let me tell you a few things you might not know about him!" I hit the keyboard to start my PowerPoint presentation. "Josh Taylor started working at the tender age of six on a commercial for Sun Shine Orange Juice. He was the little boy who showed up at school with an orange-juice moustache. Remember that commercial?" I pause, giving everyone a second to think.

Mrs. Walker taps her wrist and glares at me.

"So, the world fell in love with that little Sun Shine Orange Juice boy; they knew he was something special. A star was born, and a career was launched."

"Where was it launched, outer space?" Billy Butler says, laughing as he tosses a paper airplane, which ends up stabbing me square in the chest.

"Ow!" I wince in pain.

I hear a few kids chuckling. Billy gives Scarlett a secret nod. She winks and does that annoying, flirty giggle she always does around the guys. Suddenly, Billy pops up from his chair, both hands fly to his chest and he grimaces in fake agony … an obvious attempt to imitate me.

"That's enough, Billy! To the office, now!" Mrs. Walker points toward the door.

I glance around the classroom; now everyone is laughing (and not in a good "engaged" kind of way). Mrs. Walker checks her watch again.

Okay, I remind myself, *number four*, you-can-do-anything.com — *stay focused*.

"That's enough, class! Hannah, please continue," Mrs. Walker says, wresting back control of the class.

"Okay … so," I stammer, as the laughter starts to die down, "it was that sweet little boy with the orange-juice moustache who became the awesome musical talent we all know and love today, the one and only … Josh Taylor."

71

"Okay, Hannah, that was wonderful," Mrs. Walker says, yawning as she gets up from her seat. "So, Sam, I think you are next."

"But wait," I cry, "I wasn't done yet; I barely got started!"

"Hannah, these are supposed to be *short* presentations, no more than five minutes."

"But I —"

"Hannah, we have fifteen other students to hear from today, so I'm afraid there is no more time."

"But I have so much more … I mean, how will you mark me when I haven't even finished!"

"Don't worry, you did fine."

"Fine!" I yelp. A few of the kids are snickering. "I have to do more than fine! Public speaking is my strength! It's the one thing I'm good at! I was supposed to get the class in the palm of my hand, and I didn't even get to …"

"Hannah," she says sounding frustrated, "you got an A, now sit down!"

I got an A? Wow … I got an A! Well, of course I got an A! Public speaking is my strength; it's the one thing I'm good at! Not that Mrs. Walker heard one tenth of what I had to say. Oh well, I still got an A. I can't wait to tell Rachel!

After one more presentation about cheese or something, the bell rings. I am out of my seat like a flash and out the door, obviously not paying attention because suddenly I realize I'm like a millisecond away from smashing straight into Scarlett Hastings's stuck-up face. I slam on the brakes and kind of wobble in front of her, trying to keep balanced. She narrows her eyes, stares me up and down, and then applies a thin, shiny coat of pale pink M.A.C. lipgloss.

"Interesting presentation." She presses her lips together and pops her gloss back in her Coach bag. Anika and Missy, who have suddenly appeared on either side of her, nod in agreement. How would they know? They weren't even there.

"Oh ... thanks," I take a step back, relieved to see Rachel's head bobbing through the crowd of kids in the hallway.

"So, how did it go?" Rachel demands, rushing toward us.

Before I can open my mouth, Scarlett starts, "Well Rachel," she says, her eyes twinkling with delight, "I'd really love to tell you that Hannah did an awesome job, and that her presentation *wasn't* a complete snore-fest, but I'd be lying, and that's something I just don't do."

"That's right," Anika interjects, "she never lies."

"It's true," Missy says, wide-eyed and nodding, "she doesn't ... like, never ever."

"Oh, and I guess since we're on the subject of honesty," Scarlett continues, "I should probably tell you that your little yard sale was ... um ... actually kind of pathetic."

"Pathetic?" I rub my head, trying to absorb everything Scarlett just said.

"Yeah, Hannah, it sucked. Just like your presentation."

"Our yard sale did not suck, and I'm sure Hannah's presentation was awesome!" Rachel frowns.

"I can promise you, Rachel, it did, and Hannah's presentation was just ... sad. Oh, and by the way, I've been meaning to ask you, how's your little *ticket fund* coming along?"

"What?" Rachel looks horrified.

"Well, I heard a rumour that you two can't afford to go to the concert, so you're trying to *raise* some cash." She reaches over and pats my hand. "I hadn't realized your parents were having money problems."

I feel the red rising in my cheeks.

"Oh, that's right," she says, mockingly, "you don't even have a cellphone, do you?"

That girl knows exactly where to stick the knife in. She is pure evil.

"Oh, but don't worry, it's no big deal if you can't go to the concert. I'll take lots of pictures for you."

Rachel clenches her jaw. "Pictures?"

"Oh, I totally don't mind. You see, my father, he's pretty important, and well … how can I put this so you'll understand … let's just say … he has *connections* …" Scarlett pats her designer bag. "So, I'll be sitting in the *V.I.P.* section — that's the *Very-Important-Person* section, in case you didn't know, which is of course right next to the stage."

I roll my eyes. Rachel's face has turned crimson.

"Anyway, I'll get lots and lots of close-up shots. So now you can see the concert without actually being there, because of me. Isn't that great?"

As Scarlett blabbers away, I look over at Rachel. Her nostrils are flaring and her hands are clenched into tight fists. If I didn't know better, I'd think she was about to punch Scarlett Hastings right in her high-and-mighty face. For just a second, I let my mind drift.... *What if she actually did haul off and slug her one right in those glossy, pale-pink M.A.C. lips?* The image is happily floating around in my head when a sudden hoot of laughter brings me back to reality. It came from Rachel.

"Well actually, you misunderstand, Scarlett." Rachel says, still chuckling.

What? I look from Rachel to Scarlett, from Scarlett to Rachel. *What is she talking about?*

"Okay, this should be interesting," Scarlett says. "Go ahead, Rachel. Tell me, what did I misunderstand?"

"Well, you probably don't know that I have an aunt!" she blurts out.

"Okay … whatever …" Scarlett plucks a nail file from her bag and starts sharpening her claws.

"Well my aunt works at 98.6 The Hitz, and you know they're promoting the concert. Right?"

"Of course I do." Scarlett furrows her brow.

"Of course she does," Anika adds defensively.

"Yeah," Missy joins in.

"Well, she's hooking us up with tickets, and you know what?" Rachel glares at her. "She told me our seats are the best in the stadium! So, if there really is a V.I.P. section, then I guess we'll see you there!"

Scarlett lets out a little gasp as a look of shock registers on her face, but then slowly, an evil grin creeps across her lips. "Oh, there's a V.I.P. section, but I seriously doubt I'll see either one of you there. You see," Scarlett hisses, as she turns to walk away, "I don't believe your aunt is getting you tickets, and even if she did, I think you should know they don't let poor, boring losers with disgusting clothes from Walmart in the V.I.P. section."

"Walmart!" Rachel huffs as soon as Scarlett and her "yes-girls" turn the corner.

"Who cares? You can get some nice stuff at Walmart," I say, looking down at my cute yellow Tweety Bird T-shirt. "So, what was that all about anyway?"

"I lied," she says, shrugging.

"Yes, Einstein, I know you lied. But you never lie! Do you even have an aunt?"

"Yeah, Aunt Becky, but she doesn't work for the radio station. She works at the hospital with my dad. She's an allergy specialist," Rachel says, chuckling. "I just couldn't help myself. That girl is evil."

I nod. "Yup, she's evil all right. And she is going to torture us if we don't get those tickets."

8

Show Me the Money

Do you ever wonder what people did before Google? I mean, how did they find out anything about anything? Now, if you want to find out the population of mountain gorillas in Africa, it's just a click away; if you want to know how to make a triple-layer chocolate fudge cake, that's a click away, too, and if you want to find easy ways to make money, just type it in. And that's exactly what I did, a little over an hour ago in the computer lab.

"I have it, Rachel," I say, closing up my locker for the day. "I have the perfect answer to our problem."

"The answer to our problem is money," she says, rubbing her fingers against her thumb.

"True," I say, grinning, "and I know how we're gonna to get it."

"How?"

"Jewellery."

"Jewellery?"

"Yup," I answer, as we walk out of the school. "We're going to start a jewellery business!"

"Seriously?"

"Not just any jewellery, Rachel." I stop and look at her. "We're going to sell … friendship bracelets."

"Friendship bracelets?" She raises an eyebrow.

"People love bracelets."

"Yeah, that's true."

"Plus, they're cheap and easy to make."

"Okay, so what makes you think people will buy our bracelets?" Rachel asks.

"People will buy our bracelets because we have a gimmick," I say, crossing my arms confidently.

"A gimmick?"

"Yup, something that'll make every kid in our school desperate to have one."

"Okay, I'm listening," she says.

"So, like, hundreds of years ago, people used to make these really cool bracelets, and then they would give them to their friends as a symbol of their undying friendship and loyalty. If you accepted a bracelet, you had to promise to keep it on forever."

"Forever?" Rachel squishes up her face. "Like, never take it off? That's actually kind of gross. I mean, wouldn't it get kind of nasty after a while?"

"Well, probably, but here's the best part!" I beam. "With your promise you also got to make a wish! If you kept your bracelet on till it fell off on its own, then your wish would magically come true. Awesome, right?"

"Yeah, that's actually kind of a cool idea," she answers.

"So, I thought we might call them Wishbandz … with a *z* at the end."

"Hmmm … Wishbandz," Rachel says, smiling. "I like it!"

* * *

With that, we head to Rachel's, and get to work right away, researching patterns and figuring out what supplies we'll need. Within minutes, we meet our first obstacle — *money* — which, unfortunately, has been our problem from the start. In order to buy supplies, we need cash.

So, it's back to Google. We key in "how to find money for your business." Every site we look at points us in the same direction: *a business plan*. A business plan is really just a detailed outline of your business that you put together in order to persuade someone else to invest in your idea. In other words, we need to come up with a plan so super-professional that it will totally convince our parents to give us the cash we need to get started.

Who knew it was going to be this complicated to get tickets to a concert! Oh well, getting to see Josh Taylor will make it all worth it.

1. **Mission Statement/Goal:** To make bracelets that are *so awesome* every kid in school will be begging for one.
2. **Target Market:** Every kid in our school.
3. **Supply List:** Due to my recent history of going slightly overboard in this department, Rachel is handling supplies.

4. **Expenses:** Due to issues with my recent overspending, Rachel is looking after this part, too.

5. **Schedule:** This is where we create a timeline for buying supplies, and making and selling our Wishbandz.

So, this is our business plan. Isn't it awesome? Feel free to use it as a guide if you need to get money from your parents to start your own business. They'll be super impressed for sure!

Thankfully, our parents are pretty pumped about us "getting organized," so they happily agree to meet at Rachel's house after supper to hear our pitch.

"Ahem ..." I clear my throat and take a sip of water. "First, I would like to thank you all for coming tonight."

"Okay," Mom says, raising an eyebrow as she glances over at Rachel's mother.

"So, as you know, Rachel and I have been working really hard to earn money so we can buy tickets for the Josh Taylor concert."

Everyone nods.

"Yes, we've put a lot of effort in," Rachel adds, "but our yard sale wasn't quite as profitable as we'd hoped." She glances over at me, furrowing her brow. "So now we're exploring some new and exciting ways to earn money."

Wow, Rachel sounds so professional. Even though she's a total genius, you'd never know it by the way she *usually* freezes up when she's speaking in front of people. But not today, today she seems ... comfortable. Maybe it's because it's only our parents, or maybe she's just getting better at the whole public-speaking thing. Either way, she's doing great!

"We have developed a business plan." She picks up a pile of folders off the coffee table. "Hannah, could you please present everyone a copy?" She nods and flashes me a quick smile of what I think is relief.

I jump in. "As you can see, we've worked really hard at making our plan super detailed so you will know that your money won't be wasted. We even have a gimmick!" I smile proudly.

Rachel winks at me. "That's right, we've put a considerable amount of thought into our future Wishbandz business. If everyone would please turn to page one in your folders, Hannah will present our mission statement."

We keep taking turns presenting the business plan, explaining that Wishbandz will practically sell themselves. We end our presentation asking for our parents' trust and then their cash.

It takes a bit of negotiating and begging, but finally our parents agree to give us the money. We get to work right away buying supplies and making our Wishbandz, attaching a little tag on each one, explaining the *Legend of the Wish.*

After a couple of days of hard work, we arrive at school extra early with about twenty-five Wishbandz tacked to a corkboard. I have to say, our display rocks! Right away, people start coming over to find out what is going on. By the time the bell rings, everyone is talking about our Wishbandz, but no one is buying. At lunch, we set up our display again. We're getting lots of compliments, but apparently, no one has money.

"Oh well," I say to Rachel. "It's only day one."

Just then, Eden Payton-Patterson appears with an entourage of girls surrounding her.

If you've ever heard of someone being *strikingly*

beautiful, that would be Eden. She kind of looks like a Barbie that's come to life. Her hair is blond, almost white, and straight as a whip, and her eyes are like this weird, pale-grey colour with flecks of blue; her skin is perfect, and even in sweatpants, without a speck of makeup, she's gorgeous.

"Cool bracelets," she says, inspecting our display. Her girls eagerly nod in agreement. "I'll take ten," she adds curtly, taking out her cellphone to answer a text.

"Wow," Rachel exclaims. "You want ten?"

Eden raises a perfect eyebrow. "That's what I said."

"Um, okay. Do you want us to tie them on?" I ask.

"Duh …" She rolls her eyes, continuing to text.

One by one, each of the girls stretches out her arm, anxiously awaiting proof of her membership in the Eden Payton-Patterson Club. Each time a bracelet is tied on, Eden nods, knowing she's just secured the endless devotion of that girl. Not that she needs our Wishbandz to get their loyalty; they follow her around like adoring little puppies anyway.

As Rachel secures the last bracelet on puppy

number nine, I see Scarlett, Anika, and Missy barrelling toward us.

"OMG, as if that yard sale of yours wasn't pathetic enough, now you're trying to sell your junk at school?" Scarlett laughs as she plucks a bracelet off our corkboard. "Okay, that's just hideous!" She holds it up, turning it back and forth, and then tosses it. It lands on the ground at my feet.

"Oops ..." she says, chuckling.

Eden glances down at the bracelet in the dirt and then raises her eyes to Scarlett, who is grinning like a satisfied cat that's just finished off a helpless mouse. I'm waiting for her to start licking her lips.

"Can you believe these disgusting bracelets, Eden?" Scarlett smirks, pointing her thumb at our display. "I mean, who in their right mind would spend a dime on these cheap, loser things?"

If scowls were daggers, then Scarlett would be dead, because she just got nine *very* sharp daggers from nine *very* disgusted girls, each one holding out her arm, showing off her "disgusting" gift from Eden Payton-Patterson.

"I would, Scarlett," Eden says.

"Wait ..." Scarlett stammers, "I don't understand. You mean you bought a bracelet?"

"No, I didn't buy one," Eden replies.

Scarlett looks immediately relieved. "I knew you wouldn't buy one, of course you wouldn't. I mean ..."

"Scarlett," Eden cuts her off, "I didn't buy *just* one ... I bought ten." She points to her nine puppies' outstretched arms, and then holds up her own.

"But ... but they're ugly," Scarlett stammers.

"There is only one thing ugly here, Scarlett," Eden says calmly, "and it's not the bracelets."

The puppies all giggle. Missy gasps, and Anika bites her lip, staring at her feet, not daring to look at Scarlett.

Scarlett, suddenly realizing that she's the butt of the joke, narrows her eyes and turns toward us, glaring. Suddenly, her eyes shift toward our Wishbandz and a smile crosses her face.

"Have a nice day, girls." She turns on her designer heel and stalks off into the school with Anika and Missy trailing behind, looking confused.

"Hmmm … I wonder what she's up to now," I say.

"I'm sure we'll find out soon enough," Rachel replies with worried sigh.

9

Easy Come, Easy Go

Awesome ... that's how I'd describe our display of Wishbandz this morning. We went crazy last night and braided and beaded around thirty more bracelets. We got a lot of promises yesterday from kids who said they were going to bring cash today, so we're expecting a few more sales at least. Now that Eden Payton-Patterson (the closest thing to a celebrity in our school) and her fan club are wearing them, it won't be long before everybody wants one. That's what I'm hoping, anyway.

We set up by the front doors of the school, and like yesterday, a group of girls comes up right away. Suddenly, the crowd around us starts growing and growing until we have what seems like half the school surrounding us.

"I want the blue one," one kid says.

"I want three of those army-green beaded ones," another girl says.

"Can guys wear them?" a really cute dude from ninth grade yells out.

Rachel looks at me in amazement. "Yeah, totally!" She shouts. "Hey guys, we need everyone to line up."

Suddenly, the whole group starts shuffling themselves into a lineup.

"Wow, they listened," she whispers, flashing me a smile.

"We're in the money, Rachel," I whisper back.

"Still trying to sell your crap, I see," Scarlett says, snickering, as she, Anika, and Missy strut past the kids in line.

"Hmmm ... I don't think we're *trying* to sell anything, Scarlett," Rachel replies. "Our Wishbandz are selling themselves."

"Not for long," Scarlett whispers to us with a satisfied smirk. "The principal wants to see you in her office, A-Sap."

"Now?" I cry.

"That's what A-Sap means, loser," Anika sneers.

Rachel sighs. "She wants both of us?"

"Yes, both of you!" Missy snaps. "Wait … does she?" She looks at Scarlett for an answer.

"She wants to see both of you … now!" Scarlett looks positively blissful.

Rachel shakes her head. "What did you do, Scarlett?"

"Let's go, girls." Scarlett points to the door.

"We don't need an escort, Scarlett!" Rachel huffs.

"Oh, I wouldn't miss this for the world." Scarlett laughs as she pushes the door open.

Anika snorts. "Me neither."

Missy nods. "Yeah … um … hold it … what don't we want to miss?"

"Stay!" Scarlett holds up her hand, stopping Anika and Missy in their tracks. "Wait here until I'm done."

Scarlett rushes ahead and is gleefully holding the door for us when we arrive at the office.

"Good morning girls," Mrs. Harris says with a friendly smile. "Please come in. Have a seat."

Scarlett invites herself along.

"So, I hear you have recently become entre-preneurs," Mrs. Harris remarks.

"Entrepren-what?" I say, confused.

"Yeah, I guess," Rachel answers. "I mean, we have a product we're selling, and we have investors."

"And a business plan," I add.

"Hmm, well, taking all of that into account, I'd definitely say you're entrepreneurs," Mrs. Harris says with a little chuckle.

"Yes," I say, "entre-pren-eurs ... um ... I thought you said something else. Yeah, we're definitely entrepreneurs." I like the way that sounds ... so professional. "Would you like to see our stuff?" I add, pushing up my sleeve.

"Oh," she says, gripping my wrist. "Yes, they are quite lovely."

Rachel's face breaks into a smile; Scarlett looks beyond ticked off, and suddenly, I get it! We've been worrying for nothing. I know why Mrs. Harris invited us into her office. She's the principal and the boss, and what do bosses want from their staff? Loyalty. It doesn't take a rocket scientist to figure out that Mrs. Harris plans to buy Wishbandz for all the teachers — if she gives them bracelets, they'll feel like a special part of her team, and they'll give her their ever-lasting loyalty and devotion. Smart lady! She obviously heard how long the lineup was and didn't want to miss out. Wow, she's totally cool for a principal. This morning just keeps getting better!

"Ahem …" Scarlett coughs, tapping a large book that's found its way onto her lap.

"Oh, yes, Scarlett," Mrs. Harris stammers, "I almost forgot."

The smile on Scarlett's face has returned.

What's going on?

"So you girls call your bracelets Wishbandz?" Mrs. Harris asks.

I beam. "Yes, with a *z* at the end."

"How clever."

"Ahem …" Scarlett coughs again as she shoves the open book toward Mrs. Harris, who suddenly looks annoyed.

"Well, girls …" Mrs. Harris's face softens. "I am very pleased with the amount of effort you have put into your project. You should be very proud of yourselves."

"We are," I answer.

"Being an entrepreneur is seldom easy. There are many obstacles that can pop up unexpectedly on your way to success."

I notice that Rachel is starting to shift around in her chair, and Scarlett has suddenly transformed into an evil feline again.

"So, I'm sorry to be the one to put up your first obstacle."

"Oh, Mrs. Harris," I interrupt, "you're not our first obstacle."

"Shhhhh, Hannah," Scarlett snaps, "the principal has something very important to tell you."

"Yes, unfortunately I do." Mrs. Harris looks down at the book. "I'm afraid that it is against school board policy for students to sell goods for personal profit while on school property and during school hours. I'm sorry, girls, but you're going to have to pack up your display immediately."

And just like that, it's over.

10

The Show Must Go On

"**H**annah!" I hear Mom calling from her office.

"Coming." I let out a sigh, heaving myself off my bed.

I've been avoiding her ever since I got home from school today. I don't want deal with any questions about the business … not today.

She smiles. "How's the business going?"

"Um … great!" I lie. "Just super! Couldn't be better!" I try to force a smile, crossing my fingers behind my back.

"Really?" She tilts her head to the side suspiciously.

"Yeah … um … we have tons of bracelets made and you should see our display!"

"How are your sales?"

"Sales? What do you mean exactly?" I pick up a travel brochure with a lighthouse and a lobster on the cover.

"How many Wishbandz have you sold?"

"Well, yesterday was a pretty good day. We sold around ten."

"Yeah, you told me that. How about today?"

"Um … today was fine," I say, squeezing my crossed fingers a little tighter. "Are we planning a trip this summer?" I smile, holding up the travel guide.

"Hannah, are you avoiding my question? As an investor, I think I have a right to know how the business is going."

I fib again. "It's going fine."

"So, how many Wishbandz have you sold so far?"

"Um … well … if I add them all together, um … it would be about ten so far." I bite my lip.

"So there were no sales today?" She frowns. "I thought you said you'd have twenty or thirty more sold by now."

"Well we ran into a tiny obstacle," I finally admit.

"What kind of obstacle?"

"They shut us down at school." I look down at my feet.

"Well, *why* do you need to sell your Wishbandz at school?"

"Where else would we sell them? School is our target market, remember?"

"Well, looks like your target market doesn't care where you sell your Wishbandz as long as you are selling them." She points to her iPad and taps on the screen. "Look! You must have forty messages here, and for once they're not all from Rachel."

I plunk myself down in the chair and grab the iPad. She's right. It's not over yet!

Just then, the phone rings.

"Have you checked your messages?" Rachel squeals.

"Yeah, just checking them now," I say.

"They want our Wishbandz, Hannah!"

"Yeah, I know!"

"I don't understand it, though. I mean, how did all of these people get our contact info?"

"Well, I … um …" I stammer.

"What did you do?"

"I probably shouldn't have, but I was so ticked off with Scarlett, on the way out of the school, I tacked one of our Wishbandz on the bulletin board."

"And?" Rachel says.

"And a *little* poster with our email addresses on it."

"How little?" Rachel asks.

I laugh nervously. "It was just a piece of bristol board."

"Bristol board?"

"Well, I wanted it to be noticeable."

"I hope Scarlett didn't see it," Rachel says.

"Who cares about Scarlett? What do you think of all these orders?"

"Awesome," she answers, "but we still need a place to sell the Wishbandz. Let's be realistic; I just can't see all of these kids getting rides to our homes just to buy bracelets."

Looking through my messages, I realize she's probably right; most of these kids are bus students, and some of them don't even go to our school.

"Hey, did you get anything from Mrs. Harris?" I ask.

"I'll check," she says, pausing for a second. "Yeah, I got a message. You got one too?"

"Yeah, I did," I say, suddenly feeling weak. "Maybe she saw the poster."

"Or maybe Scarlett saw it and found some stupid rule to get us suspended."

"Suspended!" I cry.

"Hannah, you put up a poster *at the school* after we were told explicitly *not to sell at school.* Right?"

"Well, why don't I just read it," I say, clicking the message.

Hi there, Hannah and Rachel. Please stop into the office tomorrow morning before the bell so that I can return your bracelet, which I found hanging from a very large, neon green poster on our school's front lobby bulletin board today. As we discussed, it is not permissible for students to sell goods for personal profit on school property during school hours. That being said, I am very pleased with your efforts. Your bracelets are very lovely and quite unique. In all honesty, if it were up to me, I would have no issue with you selling your Wishbandz on school property. Regrettably, it's not my decision, and as another student pointed out, rules are rules. It is my sincere wish that this setback does not discourage you completely. I'm sure both of you, being as smart and innovative as you are, will figure something out. Good luck and all the best!

Mrs. Harris

P.S. I'd like to pre-order 17 Wishbandz, any design is fine as long as they are suitable for a male or a female. Please let me know when and where I can pick them up, off of school property of course.

"Hannah," Mom pops her head in the door, "Can you pass me that travel brochure off of the pile of mail on the desk?"

As I pick it up, I notice something underneath — something *very interesting*. It's a flyer. Suddenly, the solution is staring right at me.

"Rachel, did you ever hear about Christmas in October?"

"Yeah, sure! It's that craft show they have in our gym every fall."

"Rachel!" I say laughing. "This is the answer to our prayers! This is where we're gonna sell our bracelets."

* * *

Over the next week, we somehow manage to make over three hundred Wishbandz, not just for kids, but for whole hockey teams, for a church choir, for all the cashiers at the grocery store ... the list goes on and on. We send messages to everyone telling them we will be selling our Wishbandz for one night only at the Christmas in October Craft Fair.

The week flies by and before we know it, it's the big night. We haven't even finished setting up, when people start throwing money at us, trying to get first dibs on our bracelets. By the end of the evening, we manage to sell every one of our Wishbandz and we could've sold a lot more. The best and most exciting thing that happens, though, is not selling our very last bracelet, or counting up all of our profits, or finding out that we have more than enough money to buy our Josh Taylor tickets; it's meeting a Channel 7 news reporter who tells us that she is doing a TV news story on *young entrepreneurs*, and that she wants us to be a part of it! Of course, I agree for both of us right away (I mean, who wouldn't) and within minutes the camera is rolling and Rachel and I are being interviewed. Eeeeeek!

* * *

"We're here this evening with two local, young entrepreneurs, Rachel Carter and Hannah Smart," the smiling reporter, Maria, says to the camera.

The camera turns toward us. I'm grinning so much, my cheeks hurt. I must look like that stupid, smiling cat from Alice in Wonderland. I glance over at Rachel. Her eyes are like saucers.

"There has been a lot of buzz at the craft fair this evening and most of it has been around these two girls, Hannah Smart and Rachel Carter, and their *very* popular Wishbandz. So, tell me, Rachel, how did you girls come up with the idea?"

Rachel stares blankly at the camera. There is a long, awkward silence.

Maria turns to me. "Hannah, how *did* you girls come up with the idea?"

"Well," I say glancing over at Rachel, who looks like she's about to be sick, "we brainstormed a lot, and then we did some research online."

"So why bracelets? Whose decision was that?" Maria turns back to Rachel, whose face has lost all of its colour. She awkwardly giggles and points at me.

"So, it was your decision to make bracelets?" Maria asks me.

"No, it was both of our decision. This has been fifty-fifty all the way," I answer.

"So, tell me a bit more about how you came up with the idea?" Maria prods.

The camera pans back to Rachel, who's now turning green. She points at me again.

I thought that maybe after the whole busi-ness plan presentation thing with our parents, Rachel had finally kicked her fear of public speak-ing. I guess I was wrong because right now Rachel is offi-cially suffering from the worst bout of stage fright

you could ever imagine. I'm pretty sure there's no way she's going to be able to answer any of Maria's questions. I'm going to have to handle this entire interview by myself, which totally doesn't bother me. Actually, I kind of feel like a movie star on the red carpet being interviewed at the Oscars.

The camera pans back to me.

"Well, I was looking for ideas in the computer lab one day when I found out about these bracelets that they used to make, like, centuries ago. People would weave them for their friends — like old-fashioned friendship bracelets."

Maria smiles. "Neat!"

"Yeah, but they weren't just plain old bracelets; they were special."

"How so?" Maria asks

"If someone made you one, and you accepted it, in exchange you would have to make *a solemn promise.*"

"Really? What promise?" Maria turns to Rachel, giving her another chance to join the conversation.

Rachel stares ahead blankly and hunches her shoulders. The camera pans back to me.

"Well," I say, widening my eyes for effect, "you had to promise to keep it on forever … you know, as a sign of total loyalty to your friend."

"Forever?" Maria's eyes go wide as well.

"Well, eventually they'd get worn out and just fall off on their own."

"So why do you call them Wishbandz?" Maria asks.

"Well that's the most exciting part! When you get your bracelet, you make a wish, and just like back in the olden days, when it falls off, your wish will come true." I hold up my arm, showing Maria my bracelet. "Rachel made this for me. If I keep it on until it falls off, I'll get my wish!" I smile. "It's a powerful spell that's woven into each and every bracelet."

"Wow, that's really neat," Maria says, smiling. "So Hannah, you're quite the clever entrepreneur. It seems to me that a lot of this was your idea, right?"

I shake my head. "No … like I said, it was fifty-fifty all the way!"

"And tell me more about the name; did you come up with it?"

"Yeah, but …"

"So, how did you come up with it?" she asks.

"I guess it just came to me when I was in the computer lab."

"The computer lab where *you* came up with the idea in the first place, right?"

"Yeah, but ..."

"I'm sure your partner, Rachel, did her fair share, but it seems like you're the brains of this operation," she remarks, tapping my head, "Miss Smart."

"No, no ..." I stammer.

"So, what made you girls start your business in the first place? Was there a special reason?"

Now here's a question I like! I look over at Rachel to see if there's any chance she's ready to speak, but she's still in a bug-eyed trance.

"Maria, I can answer that question in two words," I say, beaming, "Josh ... Taylor."

Maria tilts her head. "Josh Taylor?"

"Well, you see, Maria, Rachel and I are Josh Taylor's biggest fans, and when we found out that he's coming to Glen Haven to do a concert, we of course told our parents right away. Well, Maria, I can tell you it was quite a shock when they said there was no way they would be paying for our tickets."

"It must have been." Maria nods supportively.

"It's a *responsibility thing*." I nod back.

"So you started the business to earn money for your tickets?"

"That's exactly what we did!" I answer proudly. "We started our business to earn money for our ..."

Suddenly, I notice Scarlett Hastings, her eyes like slits, standing directly behind the cameraman. My hand flies up to my mouth, clamping it shut as I realize what I've done. My head is spinning ... Scarlett ... Rachel's lie ... her aunt ... the fake tickets ...

Scarlett silently mouths to Rachel, "I-knew-you-were-lying."

Rachel's eyes are filling with tears. I can't believe this is happening, that I made this happen; I took over the entire interview and even worse than that ... I've ratted us out. I've ratted Rachel out.

"Well, thanks, girls. I think we have enough material to work with here," Maria says.

"That's a wrap!" the cameraman adds.

"Hannah, you did super! You're not only a great little businesswoman, but you're a natural on camera," Maria exclaims, giving my shoulders a little squeeze.

Suddenly, a crowd of kids swarms around us, and before I can get free to talk to Rachel, she's gone.

11

Attention-Grabbing,
Backstabbing Jerk of a Friend

It's official. I am the worst friend on the face of the earth. I'm so ashamed of what I've done, I couldn't even bring myself to call Rachel last night, not that she would have talked to me. Who would, unless it was to say, *Hi, Hannah, you attention-grabbing, backstabbing jerk of a friend.*

I march into school, fully prepared for the attack. I'm hoping no one saw me on TV last night. It was horrible. They barely showed Rachel at all, and worse than that, they cut out so much stuff they made it look like I was totally taking credit for everything! I'll be surprised if Rachel ever wants to speak to me again.

I rush through the lobby, trying to shield my face so that no one notices me. It's no use though;

they were all waiting. Kids start storming at me from all angles, and in like three seconds I'm surrounded. I stop in my tracks, squeeze my eyes shut and brace myself for what's coming. Everyone is yelling at me. I just want the ground to open up and swallow me so I can get out of this place.

Wouldn't it be great if that could actually happen, and a supernatural force could just suck you up and then magically drop you on some tropical island, where you'd be lying on a beautiful beach, and sipping a delicious, frozen strawberry smoothie? I don't know what I would do without these little daydreams. I think they keep me from going crazy when everything around me is falling apart. But they're only daydreams; they're not real, and no magic vacuum is going to swallow me up and spit me out in Aruba.

I open my eyes, squinting from the light. As I try to focus on the swarm of kids around me, I suddenly realize something strange is happening. It's almost like I really have been transported into an alternate universe, and that's when it hits me: these kids aren't angry, they're excited. No one is blaming me for stealing Rachel's spotlight. No one mentions the lie, either.

"How did you get to be on TV?" one kid yells out.

"They just asked me," I answer, smiling with relief.

"So, how was it? Was it fun?" another kid asks.

"Well, it was actually, really fun."

"What was Maria like?" one of the girls asks.

"She was *really* pretty, much prettier in real life, and *really* cool. She actually told me I was a natural." I do a little curtsy, kind of feeling like I'm back on the red carpet again. That's when I see Rachel from the corner of my eye, standing against the wall, watching me. Instantly, I feel the shame rising up in my chest,

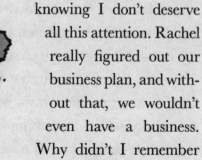

knowing I don't deserve all this attention. Rachel really figured out our business plan, and without that, we wouldn't even have a business. Why didn't I remember to say that last night? It all happened so fast. It was over so quickly. Why didn't I remember?

By lunch, the shame has risen from my chest to my throat, where it forms a huge lump that makes it hard to breathe. It won't go away, even with all the attention that has been non-stop ever since I walked into the school this morning. I know the only way I will feel better is to somehow get Rachel to forgive me. But what am I going to say to her now? She hasn't spoken to me since the interview. I don't even know if I *deserve* her forgiveness. What I do know is I feel like crap.

* * *

It's been three days and Rachel and I still haven't spoken. With every minute that goes by, I get more and more miserable. Now that my fifteen minutes of fame are over and my superstar status has died down, all I'm left with is the misery of knowing that I may have lost my very best friend in the world. We should both be so excited and planning for the concert right now. The tickets go on sale in two days and we haven't even sorted out the money from our Wishbandz. I wonder if Rachel is even still wearing hers.

"Hannah," Mrs. Harris calls out and motions to me to come into her office.

"Hi," I say solemnly, following her inside.

"I saw you on the news," she says, smiling. "You did very well."

"Oh yeah, thanks," I say, trying to manage a smile in return.

"You know, sometimes people are looking for the most interesting story, and *sometimes*, the *real* story is not the most interesting one. It's called editing."

I nod. "Editing …"

"Well, Hannah, you really are a natural in front of the camera, and it's not your fault that the story was edited to include only the most interesting parts."

"Yeah," I say hoping she's right, that it's not completely my fault.

"I'm sure Rachel realizes this too." Mrs. Harris smiles.

"Yeah, but …"

"Just talk to her, Hannah," she says as her eyes soften. "It will all work out. Trust me."

Trust her. Well, what have I got to lose? I'm miserable worrying over this. I need to fix things.

I run my fingers over the beads in the bracelet that Rachel made me. "She's my best friend," I whisper to myself, walking out of the office.

"Who, Rachel?" I hear from behind me.

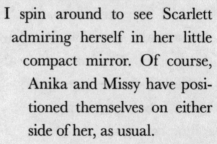

I spin around to see Scarlett admiring herself in her little compact mirror. Of course, Anika and Missy have positioned themselves on either side of her, as usual.

"She's not your best friend anymore." She smiles smugly, snapping her compact shut.

"How would you know?" I bark.

"Oh, she's not stupid, Hannah. Look at what you did," she says sneering. "Number one, you took over that whole interview. You didn't even give her a chance to speak! And then you totally bladed your little fibbing friend, exposing her lie. You know, that little story about 'her aunt' who works at the 'radio station.'" Scarlett makes finger quotes in the air and adds, "And her 'V.I.P tickets.'"

"Scarlett!" I suddenly hear Rachel yell from behind me. "Hannah did not '*blade*' me!" She uses finger quotes, mimicking Scarlett. "You knew I

115

was lying the whole time! Let's face it, I know it and you know it."

"Whatever," Scarlett says, waving her hand dismissively.

"And for your information Scarlett, Hannah did not take over that interview! She answered the questions Maria asked her and that's all!"

"If that's how you remember it," Scarlett snaps, rolling her eyes.

"It's not how I remember it — it's how it happened!" Rachel shouts.

"I was just looking out for you Rachel, I mean Hannah's obviously not that loyal of a friend."

"Obviously!" Anika squawks, clearly happy to be getting a word in.

"Yeah," Missy adds, sneering.

"She is loyal, Scarlett!" Rachel grabs my wrist just below my bracelet and pulls it up in front of Scarlett's face. "And so am I!" she barks, holding up her own.

So, right now I'm standing here, speechless, with my wrist in the air, trying to figure out what just happened. Did we just make up? Scarlett, for once, is speechless, too.

With our Wishbandz in her face, Scarlett slowly raises her narrowed eyes and locks them on mine. Her hands plant themselves firmly on her hips as she continues her stare-down. After a few moments of silent glaring, she does her signature hair flick, turns, and storms off down the hall, motioning for the bookends to follow.

12
When in Doubt, Trust Your Gut

I'm so relieved! Rachel and I are back to normal and we have a new mission: get tickets for the Josh Taylor concert, but not just any tickets. We want front-row tickets ... not an easy task, but I'm sure we can do it. After all, we are successful businesswomen. We can handle anything!

This plan is our most exciting yet! We're going to camp overnight outside the box office. This way we will be first in line when it opens in the morning — I know that buying tickets online would *technically* be easier, but Rachel and I just can't chance it. For one, thousands of people will be trying to buy their tickets online AT THE EXACT SAME TIME! — what if the website freezes up? It's totally possible ... right? Plus, sometimes our

Internet goes down for no reason. If that happened when we were trying to buy tickets, I would die! I mean, can you just imagine? Plus, buying tickets from the stadium just makes sense. I mean, wouldn't the place that's actually having the concert have the very best tickets? I'm thinking yes! Last but not least, campouts are fun, even in the winter. Anyway, *I* think it's a brilliant plan! In your face, Scarlett Hastings! V.I.P tickets here we come!

It took a little convincing, but after explaining all of the above reasons why it is *absolutely* necessary for Rachel and I to camp out for tickets, our moms finally agreed to let us. Rachel and I have loaded up the van with sleeping bags, extra blankets, pillows, a tarp, board games, a small folding table, flashlights, hand warmers, feet warmers, a cooler, tons of food, and folding chairs for the three of us (Mom insists on coming, too). We're wearing leggings under our jeans and have our heavy winter jackets, snow pants, mittens, scarves and hats all ready to go.

There is only one slight, potential problem — the weather. Looks like there might be a teensy storm tonight, nothing really, just a sprinkling of snow and a bit of wind. I'm sure it won't be that bad. Just the same, Mom is a little concerned, and she's driving, so it's up to her. I told her not to worry; I mean, we have a tarp, but she's making us wait until five o'clock for the updated forecast.

By 5:15 I'm jumping out of my skin and so is Rachel.

"Come on Mom!" I yell from the front door. "We need to get going if we want to be first in line!" I look at Rachel, frustrated. "What's taking her so long? She's driving me nuts."

"I don't think she's going to be driving us anywhere. Look …" Rachel points out the window.

"Ah, it's just a little bit of snow," I say, opening up the front door to show her. "See …" A bitter gust of wind blows through the door, whipping me in the face with ice pellets and snow.

Mom finally appears. "Shut the door, Hannah!"

"Where's your coat?" I cry, forcing the door shut against the howling wind.

Mom shakes her head. "There is a blizzard outside and it's only going to get worse as the night goes on."

"But …" I try to protest.

"But nothing!" she hollers, "I'm not going anywhere, and neither are you!"

"Mom, we have winter tires!" I yell, wiping the melting ice pellets from my face. "They're like Michelin Blizzard Blasters or some-thing. Don't you want to try them out? Look, the conditions are perfect!" I open the door again and point outside to our soon-to-be-buried-van. "Imagine us fearlessly blasting our way through the snowy streets of Glen Haven, battling the elements. The three of us braving the treacherous storm! We could make video! We could put it on YouTube and maybe Michelin would see it and want to put us in a real commercial! We'd be famous!"

"Hannah, shut the door. We're not going."

"But, Mom, we've been working all day and we're all ready to go!"

"Hannah! Drop it now!"

"Fine!" I fire back, slamming the door shut. I kick off my boots and stomp up the stairs.

"Is your mom okay?" Rachel asks when we get to my room. "She seems … I don't know … kinda cranky lately."

"Something is bugging her," I agree, shrugging out of my jacket. "I don't know, maybe it's Dad's promotion. He's working a lot, and I know she doesn't like it because I heard them arguing. I caught her crying a couple of times, too. She said it was just allergies, but I'm not stupid."

Suddenly, the lights flicker as a big blast of wind rattles the windows.

"Man this sucks," I say, plunking down on my bed.

"Well, we'll just have to buy them online tomorrow," Rachel says, yanking off her snow pants. "It'll probably be easier that way, anyway. Can you get your mom's credit card?"

"Yup. That's what she wanted me to do in the first place. She said we can just pay her back with cash."

Rachel laughs. "Awesome! We've got lots of that!"

* * *

The whole night I can barely sleep; I'm tossing and turning, afraid we are going to sleep in, even though I've checked my alarm, like, at least five times. Finally, miraculously, I fall asleep. When I wake up it's to the sound of my blaring radio. I try to unglue my eyes to see what time it is. It has to be really early because the alarm hasn't gone off. When I finally manage to pry them open, I see Rachel pacing back and forth across the floor.

"What time is it?" I whisper.

"Eleven," she says with a heavy sigh. "They're gone, Hannah, they're all gone …"

"Eleven?" I ask groggily. Then I leap out of bed, screaming, "Eleven o'clock!" "Did you get the …"

"The power went out. We slept in. The concert sold out in nine minutes."

"Nine minutes?" I say, laughing. "Yeah right!"

"Hannah." Rachel stops pacing and looks at me. "They're *all gone*."

"They're gone?"

"Gone!" she says, rubbing her forehead.

"Seriously? In nine minutes?"

"Nine *freaking* minutes," she answers, throwing her arms up in the air.

"I can't believe this, after all our hard work, after all we've been through. We're not going to get to see him?"

"This can't be happening," Rachel says, shaking her head in disbelief.

"How do you know for sure?" I ask.

"I heard it on the radio, Hannah. It's the big news of the day."

I don't think I can describe how awful we're both feeling right now, but I'm sure you can imagine. Even when I say the words out loud, it's almost too hard to believe — we're not going to see Josh Taylor.

Heartbroken, we mope in my room for the rest of the morning. It's safer in here, anyway; my parents have been arguing for the past hour. I crank up the radio, trying to drown them out just as the announcer repeats *again* how fast the concert sold out this morning.

"Can you believe it? Nearly *ten thousand* tickets gone in less than ten minutes," the DJ says, chuckling. "Unbelievable," he adds, as Josh Taylor's "Heart Attack" begins to play.

"That's it!" Rachel screams. "Hannah! Where's the phone!"

"What?" I tilt my head to the side, confused.

"The contest, Hannah!" Rachel shouts. "They're playing 'Heart Attack'!"

I'm shaking like crazy. "I think the phone's in the bed." I squeal. "You look there, I'll look downstairs."

I throw open the door, tear down the hall, round the corner, and fly down the stairs two at a time, leaping to the bottom. I am searching desperately, running all over the place when suddenly I spot Mom's cellphone on the counter, right beside her.

"Mom!" I say, choking and out of breath, "I need your phone!"

"What, Hannah? Slow down."

"PHONE!" I scream. "It's life or death!"

"What's going on?" Mom instantly panics. "Rachel! Is she okay?"

"Rachel is fine," I say dragging my nails down my cheeks. "Mom … Josh Taylor … tickets sold in nine minutes … radio contest … INEEDYOURPHONE!"

"Take it!" She thrusts it forward, looking at me like I'm a crazy person.

"Thanks!" I grab it, and tear back up the stairs, dialling as I run. I trip at the top, stubbing my toe, and the phone flies out of my hand and into the air. The searing, stinging pain pulsing through my toe is so intense, I feel like I might throw up. I bend over, grab the phone from the floor, and hobble down the hallway in agony. When I reach my bedroom, I hear Rachel speaking to someone.

"My name is Rachel Carter," she says with a shaky voice.

"And are you a big Josh Taylor fan?"

"His biggest."

"So, Rachel, have you brushed up on your Josh Taylor trivia?" the DJ asks.

"Yes," she answers, giggling nervously.

"Okay, for two amazing, front-row tickets to see Josh Taylor live in concert, can you tell me what musical instrument Josh Taylor's parents have played since they were teenagers, which Josh refuses to learn to play? Rachel … you have fifteen seconds to answer, starting now."

Rachel opens her mouth to answer, but then suddenly, grabs a scrap of paper off my desk and scribbles *French horn*. She looks at me, widening her eyes, waiting for me to nod that she's right. Instantly, I grab the paper, scratch out *French horn*, and write *trumpet*, which I'm positively sure is the right answer. OMG, I'm so happy she didn't say French horn.

"Rachel, you've got nine seconds left," the DJ says.

"Um … I'm not sure," she squeaks out, "but I think … oh …" She sighs heavily. "I'm not sure."

I furiously poke my finger on the piece of paper. I can't believe she's not saying it. *Just say* TRUMPET! *Just say it!!!*

127

"I think … it's the trumpet!" she finally blurts out.

"Ohhhh, I'm sorry Rachel, that's not the right answer. Actually, Josh and his parents all play the trumpet. Being his biggest fan, I'm surprised you didn't know that. French horn was the answer I was looking for."

13

The Big News

I don't know how much more disappointment I can take. I've been trying so hard to be positive but now I'm worn out. I'm tired of trying. I'm tired of being almost there and then failing. For a "successful little businesswoman" I don't feel very successful at all.

November is a blur, an awful grey blur of high-fives and squeals and little giggling groups of girls. Obviously, they got tickets. And then there's Scarlett and her stupid V.I.P. tickets. Honestly, I think if she goes on about them one more time, I'm going to seriously lose it. And then there is Rachel. She never did want to talk about the interview, or the lie, and she never brought up the radio contest, either. I really don't deserve her as a friend, but I'm so glad she is, because she's the only person who's keeping me from going nuts right now.

My parents have finally stopped arguing, but I still catch Mom crying every once in a while, and I hear them whispering sometimes, too, like they have some big awful secret, a horrible secret I don't want to hear. They keep saying we need to talk about something. I keep saying *later*. Honestly, I'm afraid they might be planning to get a divorce, which would be the worst thing that could ever happen, which is why I keep saying *later*. I think maybe they need more time to work things out, and as long as no one says the word out loud, there's still a chance to fix it. Unfortunately, there is no more time.

"Hannah, you can't keep saying later," Mom says with a frustrated sigh. "We need to talk."

"I'm really busy right now, I was just about to practise the guitar."

"Hannah, you don't own a guitar."

"I know that. I borrowed Rachel's."

"But why, Hannah? You don't even play the guitar."

"Exactly, that's why I need to practise!"

"Hannah, come have a seat," Mom says, patting a chair by the kitchen table.

This is it. Here it comes. I guess I can't put it off any longer.

Mom and Dad exchange a worried glance and then they both stare at me like they're waiting for me to say something.

"Okay, just say it!" I finally blurt out.

"Well," she says, rubbing the back of her neck, "we've been trying to talk to you about this for a few weeks now, but you wouldn't listen, which wasn't a big deal at the time because the decision wasn't final yet." She glances back at Dad. "But now it is, as of today."

"Final?" I ask, as a lump rises in my throat. "As of today?"

"Yes, as of today," Mom almost whispers.

Suddenly, my world is spinning. I just want it to stop. I'm not ready to hear this. I just want everything to go back to the way it was, before all the arguments and whispering and crying.

"I know," I yell, "I know what's going on. I know everything!" I shove my chair back and tear off up to my room. I try to fight back the tears, but realize it's no use, so I bury my face in my pillow, but instead of crying, I scream. I scream because I'm frustrated, I scream because I have no control over what's going on in my life, and I scream because I'm just so tired. How could I be so happy in September and so miserable now? How could my life get so totally messed up so fast?

Exhausted, I drift off to sleep until the sound of knocking wakes me up. My dad is standing in my doorway, holding a plate of supper.

"Can I come in for a sec?" he asks, smiling.

"Fine," I answer.

"I'm sorry you're so upset over what's going on," he says, putting the tray on my desk. He sits down on the edge of my bed. "Hannah, it's not going to be that bad."

"Tell me, Dad. How is it not going to be that bad?"

"Listen, this is going to be good for us. We're all going to be better off."

"Better off!" I shriek. "You're getting divorced! How could we possibly be better off?"

"Divorced?" he says, raising his eyebrows. "We're not getting divorced."

"What?"

"We're not getting divorced, Hannah," he says, shaking his head.

"You're not? Seriously? Are you sure?"

"Positive," he answers, chuckling.

I heave a big sigh of relief. "I totally thought that's what you were going to say. I was so scared."

"No, it's nothing like that."

"Well, what's going on then? Why all the arguments? Why all the whispering, and why are Mom's eyes always red?" All of a sudden I panic. "Are you sick? Is Mom sick?"

"No, no, no," he assures me, shaking his head again, "we're both healthy and madly in love, okay?"

"Okay." I nod. "So then what's going on?"

"Well, honey, you know how hard you worked to earn that money for the concert?"

"Yeah," I say, feeling more confused than ever.

"Well, when you work really hard on something it doesn't always turn out the way you expect. Sometimes it's difficult to understand how all your hard work will pay off in the end."

"I'm still waiting to understand," I say.

"What's to understand? Look how much you've learned over the last few months. When you started all this ticket business, you were disorganized and didn't know what you were doing. Look at you now, a successful business under your belt, and an appearance on TV! You handled that interview like a pro, you know?" Dad smiles and punches my shoulder. "You're a winner, Hannah."

"I feel like a loser," I mutter.

"Hannah, you never lose when you accomplish something. You become a stronger, better person."

"Yeah, I guess."

"So, just like you, I've been working hard for quite some time now trying to accomplish something. And guess what?" Dad pats my leg. "It hasn't turned out the way I expected."

"It hasn't? What do you mean?"

"Well, you know that promotion I was given a few months back?"

"Yeah."

"I worked really hard to get that job, and once I got it, I realized that it wasn't for me. I'm not good at being a supervisor. I realized I don't like being the one telling everyone else what to do; I like to be the one doing it."

"Okay, could you just tell me what is going on?" I finally interrupt.

"So, after all of the hard work and training I went through to get that promotion, I'm finally in the position to take on some exciting, new challenges."

"Dad," I say, sighing in complete and utter frustration, "would you please get to the point?"

"Well, not too long ago, an amazing opportunity just fell in my lap."

"What was it?" I ask anxiously.

"So, turns out you're not the only one in the family who's a natural in front of the camera," he says with a wink. "You are looking at the brand-new meteorologist for Channel 9 News in Maine."

"Maine?" I say, my forehead creasing. "You're going to be a weatherman on TV in *Maine*?"

"Yes I am," he says proudly.

"So, you're moving?"

"No silly," he says, laughing, *"we're* moving."

"We're moving?"

"Yup! On December thirty-first, we're headed for Maine!"

14

The Cat's Out of the Bag and Has Her Eye on Rachel

Suddenly, everything is starting to make sense ... the arguments, the long hours, the whispered conversations, and OMG ... the travel guide with a lighthouse on the front. Was it from Maine? Probably!

I can't believe we're moving. I'm leaving the only home I've ever known ... and Rachel. How can this be happening? And to make matters even worse, like, HORRIBLE, we're leaving on December 31, the night of the Josh Taylor concert. Even if Rachel and I could still somehow magically get tickets, I can't go. Dad says the plane tickets are bought and there's no changing them; the station wants him to start on January 1. Unbelievable!

I just got the best and the worst news of my

life in the space of five minutes. I don't know whether to be relieved or completely and utterly devastated. I guess I feel both really, if that makes any sense. When it comes down to it, I would rather move to Maine than see my parents getting divorced.

But Maine, what is there in Maine, anyway? I'll tell you what, lobsters and lighthouses, and none of my friends! What if my new neighbourhood has no kids? What if my school is huge? I mean it's the middle of the school year; everyone has friends already. What if they all hate me? I'm going to be friendless!

Even if I do somehow manage to make a friend, I'm sure she won't be a Rachel, because Rachels are rare, one-of-a-kind people, who just don't go randomly showing up in your life every day. What am I going to do without her? What am I going to do without my sweet, wonderful Rachel, who is always there for me no matter what?

I *really* need to talk to her and tell her what's going on. I know she'll be upset, but at least we can cry together. I roll over on my bed, grab my phone, and start dialling.

"Hi, Mrs. Carter. Is Rachel there?"

"I'm sorry Hannah, Rachel is at Scarlett's house."

"Pardon me? What?" I cough. "Did you say Scarlett?"

"Yes, she's at Scarlett Hastings's house."

"I … I don't understand," I stammer.

"Hannah, Rachel must have told you she's doing a project on fashion history."

"I don't remember," I admit.

"Well, Scarlett's mom is a fashion buyer, and she offered to let Rachel interview her."

"When?"

"Today, after yoga class. I mentioned Rachel's project to her and she just offered. Isn't that great?"

"Wow," I say, trying to imagine Rachel attempting to interview *that woman*.

"Can you ask her to call me when she gets in?"

"Sorry, Hannah, it will have to be in the morning. By the time she gets home it will be late."

How could she be with Scarlett Hastings when I need her now more than ever? This is awful!

* * *

After a night of bad dreams and tossing and turning, I wake up exhausted. I really wish I could have talked to Rachel last night. She always knows how to settle me down when I'm freaking out. I guess I could have messaged her, but this news is way too huge. I need to talk to her face to face. Only now that it's about to happen, I'm dreading it.

At school, I go to our usual meeting spot, on the bench in the front lobby. It doesn't take long before she arrives.

"Hey," I say, forcing a smile.

"Hi. Mom said you called last night."

"Yeah … um … so how were things at the Hastings Mansion?" I ask.

"Oh, pretty good. She was actually really nice."

"Who, that witchy lady? Scarlett's mom? Are we talking about the same Claire Hastings?" I say, squishing up my nose.

"Yeah, she even gave me this." Rachel holds out her arm, showing me the Bench label running up the side. "It was a sample she brought home, and Scarlett didn't want it."

"Really," I say, shaking my head in disbelief, "she didn't want it?" I mean, who would just give away a brand-new Bench jacket? Hmmm ... what does Scarlett want?

"Okay, forget about Claire Hastings," Rachel suddenly squeals. "I've got some awesome news!"

"What?"

"Guess who is in a bidding war on eBay for Josh Taylor tickets?"

"Um, you?"

"No, us! I went online last night and put a bid in. Even if we have to spend it all, we're going to that concert Hannah!" she exclaims triumphantly.

"Oh ... that was so sweet of you, Rachel, but ... but I can't ..."

"What do you mean, you can't?" she says, letting out a snort of laughter. "You're kidding, right?"

"No, I'm not kidding."

"Hannah, you're being weird. What are you talking about?"

"We're moving," I blurt out.

"No, you're not!"

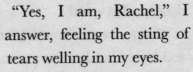

"Yes, I am, Rachel," I answer, feeling the sting of tears welling in my eyes.

"You're moving?" she cries, now panicked, "When? Where!"

"At the end of the month," I reply, as my eyes start to flood, "we're moving to Maine."

"Hannah Smart ..." says Scarlett, suddenly appearing behind us, "did I hear right?" Her grin couldn't be any more enormous as she holds her hand up to her ear and asks joyously, "Did you say you are moving to Maine?"

"Yeah, Scarlett, you heard right," I say angrily, wiping the tears from my cheeks.

Just then, Anika and Missy come rushing over. I was wondering where the bookends were.

"What's going on?" Anika demands, her eyes darting from face to face.

"Oh, terrible news, girls," Scarlett says, bringing her hand to her chest. "Hannah is moving!"

"Why is that terrible news?" Missy whispers, tilting her head, confused, "I thought we didn't like Hannah."

"Well, on the bright side," Scarlett says, her eyes gleaming, "nobody knows Hannah there, so she *might* be able to make a few friends. Well, at least for a while, until they find out how she operates."

"How I *operate*?"

"You know, how you take advantage of your friends and basically treat them like crap." She narrows her eyes. "Right Rachel? Isn't that what you were saying last night?"

Rachel's mouth falls open and she stammers, "No, no. I didn't say that. You misunderstood what I meant."

"Oh, did I?" Scarlett says shrugging. "My bad."

"What did you say?" I ask Rachel.

"I just said that you like getting attention, but I meant ..." She lets out a heavy sigh. "Well, you know how you are ..."

"Yeah, Hannah, you know how you are," Anika says smugly, crossing her arms.

"Yeah!" Missy sneers.

Scarlett runs her hand along her Gucci scarf as a satisfied grin creeps across her face. "Oh, BTW Rachel, my mother is bringing in a new shipment of designer clothes and accessories next week ... really cool samples, all hot new stuff. Anyway, she told me to invite you over, which is kind of a big deal because we'll get to pick out loot before it even makes it into the stores."

"Before it even makes it to the stores?" Anika practically swoons.

"Are we invited?" Missy asks, her eyes wild with excitement.

Scarlett puts her finger to her lips to tell the girls to be quiet. "I got these last time." She points down to her boots and beams. "They're limited-edition UGGs. Awesome, right?"

"Why does your mother want to invite me?" Rachel asks.

"She thinks you're totally smart, and a good influence." Scarlett glances over at Anika and Missy and frowns. "Anyway, you'll be needing a new BFF when Hannah moves away, and frankly, I'm getting bored —" she curves her hand at the side of her mouth and pretends to whisper "— with my current circle of friends."

"What does she mean?" Missy asks, looking all around. "Does she mean us?"

"Shut up, Missy," Anika snaps, obviously hurt by Scarlett's sudden interest in Rachel.

Although, I don't think Anika has anything to worry about; Rachel would never fall for Scarlett's tricks. NEVER EVER! I mean she's too smart for that, right? Right! At least I hope she is.

15

Never Show Up Late for a Shopping Date

Over the next few weeks, life goes on with almost the same grey awfulness as November. Only now, instead of agonizing over the concert, I'm agonizing over Maple Ridge and my future with no friends. Things between Rachel and I have been a bit weird, too. Between Christmas and getting ready for the move, I've hardly seen her or talked to her at all. Actually, I might be subconsciously trying to avoid her, maybe because every time I see her I feel so guilty. As if I didn't feel bad enough with the whole interview mess and the radio contest disaster, when she found out I'd be leaving on the night of the concert, she ended her bidding war on eBay. She said she would rather see me off at the airport than go to the concert. How many people would do that? Seriously, how could I be so selfish? I have to call her.

"Hi, Rachel."

"OMG Hannah, I'm so glad you finally called me back, but crap, I can't talk; Mom's waiting for me out in the car."

"Rachel, I need to see you."

"Me too," she cries. "Hey! I've got a great idea. Feel like spending some cash?"

"Like, yeah! When do I not?"

"True," she says with a laugh, "I think we need a shopping spree."

"A shopping spree?" I squeal, wondering why I didn't think of it myself. "When?"

"How about the Boxing Day Bonanza Sale at the mall on the twenty-ninth? Let's spend some mon-aaay!"

"I'm there!" I exclaim just as I hear Rachel's mom yell for her to get her butt out to the car *pronto*!

* * *

Our spree couldn't come quickly enough for me, and when it finally does, I'm, like, crazy excited! Everywhere I turn there are Boxing Day sales. I'm supposed to be meeting Rachel in the food court in five minutes, but right now I'm eying an awesome striped scarf on an American Eagle sale table and it's 75 percent off! The problem is some blond chick is now trying it on. I *really* want that scarf. Suddenly, she turns around — it's Eden Payton-Patterson and she's got my scarf.

"Um, do you want something?" She purses her lips, frowning.

"Um, no."

"Well then, why are you staring at me?"

"I wasn't."

"Yes you were. Are you a stalker?"

"No … um … I just like the scarf."

"Ew," she says pulling it off her neck, "this thing?" She rolls her eyes and tosses it back on the table.

Before she can change her mind, I grab the scarf and race for the cash. There are two people ahead of me; one is returning a huge bag of clothes, and the other is having problems with her MasterCard. It takes ten full minutes for the two in front of me to finish. When it's finally my turn, I throw the scarf down on the counter with a twenty. The girl then slowly scans the bar code, counts out my change, and starts neatly wrapping my scarf in tissue paper. She's taking forever!

"No paper," I finally yell, "I'll wear it!" I grab the scarf, yank the price tag off, and throw it around my neck as I tear out of the store. I race through the mall and hop on the escalator, squeezing my way up through passengers until I reach the top. When I arrive at the food court, I'm relieved to see Rachel right away. It looks like she is in the middle of a deep discussion with someone. That's good; maybe she won't notice that I'm late ... Holy crap! It's Scarlett Hastings. What is she doing here? I try to wave to Rachel to let her know that I'm on my way, but she can't see me. She's totally absorbed in her conversation with Scarlett. When I get a little closer I can hear them.

"You know, you'll be better off without her."

"What?" Rachel says.

"We could have been really great friends if it weren't for Hannah. You know, she hasn't let you out of her sight since the minute you moved here, don't you? Haven't you noticed that she sticks to you like glue?" Scarlett snipes.

"She doesn't stick to me like glue!" Rachel exclaims.

"Really?" Scarlett says, folding her arms in front of her. "Did you know that Hannah didn't have any friends before you came along?"

"No."

"Well, she didn't, and do you know why? Because she's selfish!"

"Selfish?" Rachel echoes, confused.

"Look at how late she is, Rachel! She's *so* self-centered, thinking her time is more important than yours!" Scarlett taps her watch. "She makes you wait a lot, doesn't she?"

"Not really ... sometimes," Rachel says, glancing around the food court.

"Wasn't she supposed to be here, like, a half an hour ago?"

"Actually, twenty minutes ago." Rachel says, looking down at her wrist.

I yank up my sleeve to check the time. Am I really twenty minutes late? I have to get over there!

"Well, hello, Hannah," Mrs. Harris says, suddenly appearing beside me. *Where the heck did she come from?* "Doing a little last-minute shopping before the big trip?"

"Yeah... yeah a little bit." I stammer, feeling more desperate than ever to get to Rachel.

"How was your Christmas?"

"It was good," I answer, scratching my head nervously.

"And you're leaving in a couple of days?"

"Yes."

"Hannah? Are you okay?" Mrs. Harris tilts her head.

"Yes, I'm okay, I'm just late."

"Well, I'm so glad I got to see you before you left." She leans over and gives me a big squeeze.

"Safe travels!"

"Okay, Mrs. Harris, and thanks again for everything," I say, hugging her good-bye.

When I look back, Rachel and Scarlett are gone. This is not good! Where are they?

After a frantic scan of the food court, I finally spot them sipping iced cappuccinos at a table in front of Starbucks.

As I approach, I hear Rachel's voice.

"You're right. Hannah is the most selfish person I know. I'll totally ditch her and go to the concert with you. I mean after all, I'd be crazy to pass up those V.I.P. tickets right?" I gasp in shock.

Rachel looks up, panic-stricken. "No, no, you don't understand, Hannah!" she cries.

Scarlett looks positively blissful. She crosses her legs and taps Rachel's boot with her foot. Suddenly, I notice the brand new pair of UGGs on Rachel's feet. And at that moment the reality of the situation becomes as clear as the word Prada on Rachel's new bag. I've been replaced.

16

Go Means Go

It's New Year's Eve. I never could have imagined it, but I just want to get this day over with so I can get on with my life in Maple Ridge.

I haven't spoken to Rachel since the mall. This whole situation seems so unreal. She's tried to call me, but there is really nothing more to say. She's right. I've been the most selfish person on the face of the earth. I'd like to say that I'm glad she's at the concert, but every time I imagine her and Scarlett together, sitting in the V.I.P. section, wearing their designer outfits, with their designer boots and designer bags, I feel a little ill.

We've been standing in line at the airport for what seems like forever.

"What a crappy way to spend New Year's Eve," a kid in line says to the guy next to him.

"Tell me about it," I find myself throwing in.

The kid stares at me and then looks away, shaking his head. *Was he scowling?* What a weirdo.

Suddenly, my attention is drawn to some crazy person darting back and forth through the crowd. I'm shocked when I discover who it is.

"Hannah!" Rachel yells, gasping for air, "I'm so glad you haven't left!" She thrusts a Josh Taylor concert T-shirt at me.

"How was the show?" I ask, looking down at the shirt.

"Hannah, I didn't go to the concert with Scarlett," she says in between pants.

"Whatever." I shrug.

"Really, I didn't!"

"I heard you at the mall, Rachel; I heard you say you'd be crazy not to go. I heard everything."

"I was being sarcastic, Hannah."

"Sarcastic?"

"Couldn't you tell by my voice? I just wanted Scarlett to hear how *stupid* she sounded so I was repeating back every word she said."

"Really?"

"Oh my gosh, Hannah, yes really!" Rachel says, exasperated. "I mean *come on*, can you seriously imagine me as one of the bookends?"

"What about the UGGs and the Prada bag and all the designer clothes?"

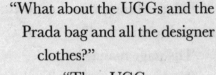
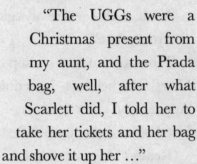

"The UGGs were a Christmas present from my aunt, and the Prada bag, well, after what Scarlett did, I told her to take her tickets and her bag and shove it up her ..."

"Rachel," I say with a gasp, "you didn't!"

"Yes, I did," she says giggling.

"What about the Bench jacket?"

"Oh, I'm keeping that!" She smirks. "I figure I earned it."

"Then where did the Josh Taylor T-shirt come from?"

"Well, I went to the concert, but only because of my aunt."

"Your aunt? The one who gave you the UGGs ... the allergy specialist?"

"Yup, that's the one," Rachel answers. "Well, Aunt Becky was working today, and just happened to be in the emergency room when an ambulance brought in ...get this ... Josh Taylor's new stage manager!"

"His stage manager?"

"Yeah, with a severe allergic reaction."

"From what?"

"From a clam or a scallop or something," Rachel says incredulously. "Apparently, her airway was closed off and she almost died!"

"Really?" My jaw drops.

"Yeah, and my aunt saved her life!" Rachel exclaims. "Well, this lady was so grateful that she gave Aunt Becky tickets and souvenir programs and Josh Taylor glow sticks and T-shirts and even backstage passes."

"Seriously?"

"Yeah, we got to sit in the skybox with all these big shots in fancy suits, and they served us snacks and drinks and slushies and ... oh ..." Rachel's smile suddenly falls as she glances down at the Josh Taylor shirt in my hands. "I wish you could've been there, Hannah."

I know from the sadness in her eyes that she really means it.

"Wow, did you see Scarlett there?" I blurt out, trying to lighten the mood (not to mention, I'm really curious).

"Yeah, I saw her … through my binoculars."

"In the V.I.P. section?" I can't help but sneer.

"No," she says with a snort of laughter, "in the nosebleed section!"

"*Nosebleed* section?"

"Yeah, like the worst seats in the whole place!"

"Really? What happened?"

"Well, from what I hear, at the last minute her dad's *connection* fell through, so she had to buy her tickets on ebay at triple the price."

"Karma," I say.

"Total karma," she agrees, nodding.

"Wait … how did you even get here?" I ask suddenly.

Rachel points behind her. "My mom is waiting outside with the car. She didn't want to pay for parking and told me to be quick." She shrugs, grinning. "But whatever. I won't be seeing you again for, like … I don't even know how long!"

"I know!" I look down at the floor, avoiding her eyes. I don't want to cry.

"So, what was it like backstage?" I ask. "Did you meet him?"

"No …" Rachel shakes her head with a smile. "We left before the last song."

"But why?" I look at her, confused.

"That's a stupid question," she says, yanking my hair playfully. "We had to beat the traffic so we could make it to the airport in time."

"What?" I half whisper, shaking my head, "but you could have met him … Josh Taylor."

"Maybe," she says with a shrug, "but Josh Taylor hasn't been my very best friend in the entire world for the past five years, has he?"

"It's time to go, Hannah," Mom says, softly.

Rachel looks down at her feet, rocking back and forth. "See ya later, Movie Star," she says, glancing up at me.

"See ya, Brainiac," I whisper back. I really want to hug her but know if I do, I'll lose it and start bawling, and I've already done enough of that.

"Hannah, it's time to go." Mom motions with her hand.

Rachel looks back down at her feet, and I know she's feeling the exact same thing as me. I don't know when I'll see her again, or if I'll *ever* see her again. What am I going to do without her? Suddenly, I can't help myself and wrap my arms around her. "I'm gonna miss you, Rachel … so, so much."

"You're gonna miss your plane, loser," Rachel says, grinning, knowing I always laugh when she calls me that.

"Whatever," I say, managing a little chuckle.

That's *why* I'm going to miss her so much. She knows me. Thank god, too, because I was on the verge of bursting into tears, and a big embarrassing scene is something I definitely don't need right now.

"Message me when you get there," Rachel says, wiping away a tear. With one final wave, she turns and walks away, disappearing into the crowd.

* * *

"So, wasn't that nice of Rachel to come and see you off?" Mom dabs her eye with a tissue as we pass through security.

"Yeah, it *was* great," I say, trying to muster a smile.

"So, I know this is your first time flying and you're a bit nervous about the flight …" Mom says, putting her hand on my shoulder. "So, I don't want you to panic when I tell you this."

"Tell me what?" I yank my shoulder away, wondering why on earth she would tell me not to panic when she knows that's exactly what I am going to do.

"Well …" she says, hesitating.

"Well what!" I almost yell.

"We're not going to be sitting together," she quickly blurts out.

"We're not going to be sitting together?" I say, grabbing her sleeve, "but at least you'll be in the same row. Right?"

Mom grimaces. "Not exactly."

"Well, how far apart are we going to be? I mean, I've never been on a plane before, and what if there's turbulence and I need oxygen?" I snap. "Isn't it the mother's job to put on their child's oxygen mask? Who's going to put on my oxygen mask?"

Suddenly, I notice people are looking at me. One of them is the boy who was scowling at me earlier. And he's laughing! How RUDE!

"Hannah, you'll be just fine," Mom assures me. "You won't need extra oxygen, and if you're worried, just review the safety instructions in the seat pocket in front of you. Okay?"

"Fine," I huff, casting my worst glare at that stupid, smirking boy.

As I make my way slowly down the ramp toward the plane, my heart starts racing. By the time I reach the entrance, it's almost beating out of my chest.

"Okay, here we are," the flight attendant says. "Just put your carry-on up here." She taps the overhead bin to open it.

Great! How am I supposed to fit my bag up there? It's already full! I shove it in as hard as I can, but I'm trembling so much, I don't have any strength. I try to manoeuvre the other bags filling the bin to make room for mine, but they won't budge. In desperation, I look down the aisle for the flight attendant. The line of passengers is beginning to back up and everyone is staring at me … again. I start shoving my bag in harder, trying frantically to make it fit, when it finally decides to fight back, and lands on my seat with a thud.

The guy in the chair next to me suddenly looks up. It's him!

"Oh, it's you." He smirks, taking out his earphones. "Need any help?"

"Absolutely not!" I frown, grabbing my bag off the seat. I look back at the growing line of passengers and start desperately trying to shove it in the bin again.

"Looks like you're having a little difficulty there. Are you sure you don't need any help?" He points up at my bag, half hanging out of the already-overstuffed bin and laughs.

"Positive!" I glare, ramming it in as hard as I can.

"I think that bin is full," says the flight attendant, who has magically reappeared. "Why don't you try this one?" She taps open another bin.

After my bag is safely stowed overhead, I plunk myself down in my seat, immediately secure my seatbelt, and grab the safety instructions from seat pocket.

"I'm A.J.," the annoying boy says, holding out his hand, expecting me to shake it.

I look at his hand and scowl. "I'm sorry, but I'm kind of busy familiarizing myself with the safety procedures. I don't have time to socialize right now."

"Oh, pardon me then." He rolls his eyes, laughs, and then starts playing on his iPod.

* * *

"Flight attendants, please prepare for takeoff." I hear the captain say over the intercom. Suddenly, the plane begins to move. A little scream escapes me. *Okay, just stay calm. I can do this!* The plane slowly makes its way to the runway. So far, so good. This is it; there is no turning back now. I grip the arms of my chair and close my eyes. Suddenly, the engines start to roar, and, without warning, the plane shoots down the runway at lightning speed. It's going so fast that the g-force is pressing me back in my seat. I don't like this. I don't like this at all!

"I changed my mind! I'm not ready!" I yell over the roaring engine. "Tell the captain to turn around. I want to go back!"

No one is listening. A.J. has his ear buds in. He definitely can't hear me. He's too busy listening to music on his iPod! OMG! His iPod is on! They told us no personal electronics during lift-off! Electronics mess with the controls! I can't believe how inconsiderate this guy is! He's going to crash our plane! I can't let this happen. I grab the iPod out of his hand, but before I get to turn it off, the plane starts lifting off the ground.

"Nooooo!" I scream.

We're not lifting fast enough; the tail is going to hit the ground! I'm going to die right here, right now, on this very plane! I'm too young to die!

Suddenly, we're in the air. We made it! Phew!

OMG! The iPod! It's still on, and he's trying to get it back! There's no way he's getting it!

"I need to turn this off!" I yell, furiously pressing down on the power button.

A.J. finally yanks it from my grip, "What's the deal?" he says, frowning.

"Turn it off!" I shriek. "No personal electronic devices during takeoff! The flight attendant told us! Don't you remember?"

"Nope." He laughs. "Guess I was busy trying to mastermind a way to take down the plane ..." he smirks annoyingly "... with my all-powerful iPod."

"Turn that thing off!" I screech again.

"Okay," he says calmly, "I'll turn it off, but you need to relax! Do you really think that this little thing could make the engine explode?"

"Yes, I do," I say with a confident nod of my head. "And thank god I noticed, or we might all be dead."

"Well thank you for saving us," A.J. says sarcastically.

"My pleasure," I growl.

* * *

About twenty minutes into the flight A.J speaks again.

"Could I get by, please?" he asks, starting to get up.

"No," I answer.

He frowns. "What do you mean ... no?"

"I mean I'm not moving."

"Okay," he huffs, "I really need you to move."

"Sorry, I'm not taking off this seatbelt."

"Why ... are you still nervous?" He asks, grinning.

"Of course I'm not nervous!" I snap. "I'm a very experienced flyer!"

"Really?" He raises an eyebrow. "You seem nervous to me."

"Really?" I sneer. "Why do you think I seem nervous?"

"Well, maybe because you read the safety instructions at least eleven times, or because you demanded to wear your life jacket, 'just in case,' or because you quizzed all three flight attendants on their knowledge of emergency landing procedures, or maybe I think you're nervous because at one point you screamed out, 'Oh my god, we're going down ... we're all going to die!'"

"I only said that because I was startled by the sudden turbulence!" I huff.

"It wasn't turbulence," he says, shaking his head. "Some big guy bumped into your chair."

I blush. "Oh …"

"Now will you please move? I really have to go."

"Oh," I say, suddenly understanding, "you have to gooooo."

"Yeah." A.J. scowls. "Look, why don't you use my iPod for a while? I think it's pretty safe now that we're up in the air."

"Hmm …" I say, considering his offer.

"Look, I've got a bunch of cool stuff on there. You should be able to find something to occupy your mind until we land."

"Um … thanks," I stammer, taking the device.

"So, can I get by?" he asks, with a dimpled smirk.

"Sorry!" I blush again, unclipping my seatbelt.

Well, I guess he's not that bad. I mean, it's pretty nice when a person just offers their iPod to a random stranger, especially when that stranger stupidly packed her iPod in her checked luggage.

"Thanks," he says, flashing a grin as he edges past me in my seat. "What did you say your name was?"

Wow, his eyes are sooo brown. "I didn't." I smile.

"I'm A.J.," he says, holding out his hand again.

I give it a quick shake. "I'm Hannah."

His grin widens as he pushes a piece of sandy blond hair from his eyes. "Well, it's nice to *finally* meet you, Hannah."

When A.J. gets back to his seat, he starts showing me all the apps on his iPod, and before I know it, we're landing. We're in Maine, the land of lobsters and lighthouses … my new home.

* * *

While Mom and Dad are collecting our luggage, I do a quick scan of the airport. I don't see him anywhere. Well, I guess that's it then; he's gone … I wonder how old he is … maybe a year older than me? Why didn't I ask him?

"Hannah, isn't that the boy you were sitting with on the plane?" Mom points to the luggage carrousel.

"Where!" I say, whipping my head around, possibly looking a little too eager.

"Over there." She points at an old guy.

"Mom, that's an old man," I say, hoping she doesn't notice my disappointment.

"No, behind the old man," she says, pointing again. "You two were sure talking up a storm."

Suddenly, I spot him. He's lifting his bag from the conveyor belt. I thought I'd never see him again. I wonder where he's from. Why didn't I ask him? Actually, I didn't ask him anything. Why didn't I? Wow, he's got nice hair.

Suddenly, I'm feeling weird. My cheeks are warm, my armpits are itchy, and I'm sweating. I never sweat! It must be awfully hot in this airport.

Just then, he starts walking toward me. My heart is racing even faster than it did when I got on airplane, and I can feel the blood pulsing in my ears. Have I completely lost it?

He's getting closer. Now my cheeks are burning … like, on fire! My legs are wobbly and I'm actually feeling kind of dizzy.

Okay, I'm just being stupid. I mean he's only a boy … a boy, who's actually really, really cute! What's wrong with me?

I'll pretend I don't see him. I'll look at the ground. My shoe is untied. Good! I'll tie my shoe.

Oh no, he's right in front of me. I'll pretend not to notice. Maybe he'll go away.

"Ahem …"

I look up. "Hi there," I blurt out like a complete idiot. I'm sure my face is beet red … like, crimson. This is awful!

He points at my foot. "Your shoe is untied."

"Oh yeah, I know," I say with a little giggle. Okay now, how stupid did that sound? And why did I giggle? I'm making a complete fool of myself.

"Well, are you going to tie it?"

"Yeah … I will later," I say, glancing down. *Why, why, why did I say that? What a moron!*

"Okay, whatever." He shrugs, laughing. "Can I have my iPod back?"

"Oh, oh … sorry." I take it out of my pocket. "I guess I forgot to give it to you. It's been a big day."

"No problem," he answers, flashing another grin. "Hey, are you that wish-bracelet girl I saw on the news a while back?"

I smile. "Yeah, only they're called Wishbandz." And then add, stupidly, "with a *z*."

"Okay …" He snickers. "I thought you looked familiar."

"Yeah." I nod, not knowing what else to say.

"So … my iPod?" he says, holding out his hand.

"Oh, sorry!" I pass it to him, feeling his fingers lightly brush over mine as he takes it. My legs are threatening to give out any second.

"Cool! Well, maybe I'll see you around, Bracelet Girl," he calls out, popping his iPod into his pocket as he walks towards the exit.

"They're called Wishbandz!" I yell back, correcting him *again* like a complete loser.

"Whatever!" He calls back, laughing, as the doors close behind him.

17

Gabby

Turning into our new neighbourhood, I get a strange feeling, but it's a good strange feeling. It's hard to explain, but it's kind of like I can breathe again. Now that I know my parents are fine, the concert has come and gone, and the whole awful mess with Rachel is over with, I only have my future to focus on. I have to admit I'm a little bit curious, and a little excited, too.

As we drive along, I start noticing that this neighbourhood doesn't look too different from the one I just left. I'm anxious to see our new house. My parents came over a couple of weeks ago and sorted out all the furniture and stuff. Mom says she's pretty positive that I'll be happy with this part of the move.

As we round the corner, Mom suddenly squeals, "There it is!" She points to a house about the size of Scarlett's. It's a pretty, two-storey Victorian-style brick house with a big covered porch and white pillars. The front door is massive and has a huge Christmas wreath on it. On each side of the door are black wrought-iron urns holding spruce boughs and bright red holly. The whole house is covered in soft, white, twinkling lights, making it look just like a Christmas card.

"The wreath was a gift from the neighbours," Mom says, pointing across the street to a beautiful little house that looks like it's made of gingerbread. I can hear music coming from inside. It sounds like they're having a party.

"Oh, and I almost forgot to tell you," she adds as we pull into our new driveway, "they have a daughter and she's your age! How neat is that?"

"Neat …" I mutter, suddenly filled with dread. What if I'm moving next door to another Scarlett, and what if she has evil friends and what if they all hate me? Ever since Dad dropped the awful "we're moving to Maple Ridge bomb," I've been kind of obsessing over the whole making-new-friends thing. Let's face it — I've never been a *friend magnet* like Eden with a throng of girls trailing after me.

As soon as the front door to my new house is unlocked, I run in, kick off my boots, and leap up the stairs to find my room. I run down the hall, throwing doors open … the bathroom … my parents' room … the guestroom (I hope) … and then, jackpot! My room …

My first impression … OMG. Okay, where do I start? Well, at first glance, my new room is more awesome than you could ever imagine. The walls are painted the most perfect shade of light purple that Mom says is called Twilight Mist. My bed is beautiful! It's a huge, cream-coloured sleigh bed, covered with a gorgeous, silky, pale-pink duvet with mauve, silver, and hot-pink sequined throw pillows. In the corner of my room, there's an amazing silver floor lamp that comes up and arches over with a really cool shade made of dangling crystals. Against the wall, beside my lamp, there's a big cream-coloured desk that matches my bed. Against another wall there's a gigantic mahogany bookshelf that's filled with books, a few of them that I've been dying to read. I'm guessing the books must have belonged to the girl who used to live here before. Wow, she has good taste. Beside the bookshelf is a door leading into a huge walk-in closet, complete with shelves and compartments, and even a full-length oval mirror! Beside my closet is my very own en suite bathroom with a walk-in shower, and it's totally colour-coordinated with my room! Seriously, am I dreaming? I really hope not because beside the bathroom, is a ladder, and at the top of the ladder is a loft, an amazing little loft! At one end, sitting on top of a pretty lilac-purple shag rug, are a couple of cushy pink beanbag chairs, and at the other end, attached to the wall, is the most beautiful thirty-two-inch LCD TV that I've ever seen because it's mine! Can you believe it? I have my own little loft living room!

"Do you like it?" Mom asks, poking her head in the doorway.

"Come on, Mom! Are you kidding?" I squeal, sliding down the ladder.

"What do you think of the loft?"

"I just can't believe this is my room!" I answer, looking around, trying to soak it all in.

"What do you think of the walls?"

"Oh, Mom," I say, suddenly realizing that she's tacked up every one of my Josh Taylor posters. "I can't believe you brought them."

"Well, come and see the rest of the house!" She grabs my hand and pulls me into the hallway.

At that moment, the doorbell rings.

"Oh, that must be Gabby," Mom says, like I should know who she's talking about. "Well, go answer the door."

I'm halfway down the stairs when the doorbell rings again. I open the door, and standing there is a girl around my age with a head full of shoulder-length, dirty-blond curls, rosy cheeks, and pretty brown eyes rimmed with thick eyelashes. She's wearing a silver-coloured parka over a black sequined cocktail dress. She's rubbing her hands together and stomping her furry grey boots, trying knock off the snow.

"Hi there. I'm Gabby, your next-door neigh-bour." She comes into the house and closes the door behind her. "Actually, my full name is Gabriella, but you can call me Gabby. You must be Hannah?" She flashes a huge smile with just about the cutest dimples I've ever seen.

"Hi Gabby," I say.

"So guess what!" she suddenly blurts out. "My best friend used to live here, seriously, in this very house. I miss her like crazy. Actually, I've been super depressed ever since she left, but when I heard you were coming, I started feeling better, like way better, and I've been dying to meet you ever since." She looks at me, her eyes sparkling, as her face breaks into another huge grin.

Suddenly, I desperately miss Rachel. Gabby's grin is a Rachel grin, if I ever saw one. But Rachel's back in Vermont and I really have to make *new* friends. Gabby seems nice; she's a fast talker, but she's friendly and she seems pretty excited to meet me.

"So, how do you like your new room? It's awesome, right?" Gabby squeals. "I helped pick out the colours and I even helped paint it, which took a long time because it's such a big room. Totally worth it though, right? So what do you think of the loft?"

"The loft …" I spit out as fast as I can. "It's really cool! Do you want to come up?"

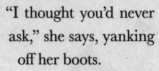

"I thought you'd never ask," she says, yanking off her boots.

"So what do you think of the rest of the house?"

"I haven't seen it yet; we just got here, like, fifteen minutes ago."

"Oh yeah, right!" She opens the front closet and throws in her parka. "I'll show you around. Come on!" she cries, motioning for me follow.

She whisks me in and out of every room in the house. The last stop is my bedroom. She swings open the door. "*Oh my gosh!*" she yells, stopping in her tracks.

What? What did I do? Is it the posters? Is she mad about the tape messing up the walls!